PINNED DOWN!

Cole rose from behind the boulder, sighting the Winchester on the first movement he saw; one of the attackers aiming a Henry rifle right at him. Both men shot, but only Cole's bullet found its mark, piercing the attacker's throat, dropping him behind the rocks.

Cole stroked the lever and looked for his next target. A young kid, not more than eighteen, came from cover, raising a rifle. Cole fired quickly, winging the kid's right shoulder, making him drop the rifle in front of him. Cole levered and fired again, striking the kid's gut. Blood splattered the rocks behind the boy, but he continued to reach for the weapon, which lay just out of his grasp. Cole levered, the spent shell ejecting over his shoulder, and fired once more, mercifully ending the young man's life with a slug between the eyes.

Dust sprayed up from the boulder top. The whir of a spinning bullet passed by his ear. Cole fired into the cloud and waited for a cry. He heard nothing. As the screening dirt blew away, the figure of a man took shape. It was a man with a rifle aimed at him.

D0768028

Independence Public Library
311 Monmouth Street
Independence, Oregon 97351

DANGER RIDGE

2128 8920

TIM McGUIRE

LEISURE BOOKS NEW YORK CITY

To My Parents

To my mom, Jeanne: You always loved a good Western. And to my dad, R.J., who was the only one who truly believed I could really do this.
The bumblebees were flying during this one.

A LEISURE BOOK®

July 1998

Published by

Dorchester Publishing Co., Inc.
276 Fifth Avenue
New York, NY 10001

If you purchased this book without a cover you should be aware that this book is stolen property. It was reported as "unsold and destroyed" to the publisher and neither the author nor the publisher has received any payment for this "stripped book."

Copyright © 1998 by Tim McGuire

All rights reserved. No part of this book may be reproduced or transmitted in any form or by any electronic or mechanical means, including photocopying, recording or by any information storage and retrieval system, without the written permission of the Publisher, except where permitted by law.

ISBN 0-8439-4410-2

The name "Leisure Books" and the stylized "L" with design are trademarks of Dorchester Publishing Co., Inc.

Printed in the United States of America.

ACKNOWLEDGEMENTS

To Joy, Cameron, Ryan, and Erin for putting up with me through all of this, I love you. Teachers JoAnne Pickett, Carol West, and Betty Jones who said I'd do something special someday, I did it. Thank you to my sisters and brother, all my family and friends who offered suggestions with their support and encouragement which drove me to finish this, and an unpayable debt of gratitude to *DFW Writers' Workshop,* who took this daydreaming storyteller and turned him into a writer.

Danger Ridge

Wednesday, July 30, 1879

Dearest Mother,

Please forgive me for what I have done to you. I know how you must be worrying. Please don't be angry with me. I pray you will understand why I had to leave home.

I will let you decide whether to show this letter to Daddy. I know of his disapproval of John and of what I am doing, but I feel compelled to follow through with this. John is my husband. When I received his wire to join him, I knew it was the right thing to do.

His venture in the silver mines of Colo-

rado isn't the folly that Daddy believes. From what I have observed, it is one of the most prominent industries in the West.

I apologize for the way I obtained the money, but not for taking it. It is my money, and I assure you it is securely in my control. According to John, the funds will be needed to start a new life here.

I know you're worried about your only child traveling alone to such a faraway place as Colorado. But I am a twenty-five-year-old woman now and I am joining the man I married to be at his side.

The land here is beautiful. Wondrous snowcapped mountains, larger than any I have seen before, and the people I have met have all been very kind. However, I realize life here won't be as I knew it in the East. One can live without city restaurants and visiting friends' estates. At least there are no savages like those that Daddy described. And yes, there are separate necessary rooms as well; another fact he was mistaken about. Although this hotel has two of the few that are indoors.

I regret the time it has taken me to write. However, this is the first opportunity I've had to do so in the twenty-eight days since I departed Baltimore. The trip has been long. It has taken a toll on my body, but not my spirit. Tomorrow my train departs Denver for the West. In two days' travel I will finally be with John.

You both will be in my thoughts and prayers. I miss you both terribly, but my destiny is with him. I know I will be safe. Be happy for me. I can't wait.

Your loving daughter,
Claire

Chapter One

The 5:15 screamed its arrival into Platte Falls.
The engine bellowed a white blanket of steam
on the tracks as the locomotive slowed to a stop.
Claire Rhodes stepped onto the depot platform,
her open parasol sheltering her fair skin from
the blazing sun. Her coal-black hair was pinned
up under a summer bonnet. A glance in the
train car window reflected the soot and dust
marring her cheeks. Quickly she brushed away
the blemishes of the two-day journey from her
face and Parisian blue taffeta dress. Her fingers
centered the gold-mounted ruby brooch on her
collar. She took a deep breath in anticipation of
her first sight of her husband in nearly a year.

As she made her way to the end of the platform, she looked for John. She failed to spot his face in the crowd. A porter carted her two bags and large trunk next to her. She thanked him and paid a gratuity for his service.

"Are you Mrs. Rhodes? Mrs. John Rhodes?"

She turned to face a large, burly man with five-day-old whiskers surrounding a wide grin. He picked up the bags and was quickly joined by two other men, one tall and slim and the other short and stocky. The trio removed their hats and smiled.

Claire nodded.

"Call me Jeb, this here's Caleb, over there's Little Fred. We was told to come bring you to Mr. Rhodes's mine."

Claire was shocked to learn John wasn't there to greet her, although it wasn't the first time he'd disappointed her. She looked at her modest gold band. "Where's my husband?"

"Oh, he's back at the mine, makin' sure nobody don't steal any of the ore, or maybe even jump the claim. That's why he sent us for you."

She put her hands on her hips, becoming more disgusted with every word she heard. Her disbelief at John's callousness soon gave way to her lack of options in the situation.

"Will you load that in their wagon?" she asked the porter, pointing at the trunk.

"We didn't bring no wagon," Jeb said. "There's no roads for one where we're goin'. We can come back with a mule for that."

"Then how do you plan to get me there?"

"We brought a mare for you, ma'am," Caleb answered. "A real gentle one."

After a moment's pause, she relented. "Very well." She turned to the porter. "Will you please hold my trunk here until we can come back for it? Please make sure it is handled with care," she said, opening her small purse. "There are items in there very precious to me." She held out a silver coin and placed it in the porter's waiting hand. The man tipped his cap and carted the trunk back to the station.

Claire stepped down off the platform, refusing Jeb's outstretched arms, and walked toward the center of town. Her graceful steps were occasionally interrupted as she was forced to avoid the numerous mudholes. She hadn't come this far to soil her hem or her buttoned suede shoes.

"I hadn't planned on horseback riding. How far is it to Mr. Rhodes's mine?"

"Oh, it's not too far, maybe two days' ride if the weather holds," Little Fred answered.

"Two more days!"

Jeb threw a look at Little Fred that could have knocked him down. "It ain't that far, Mrs. Rhodes. Besides, it's real pretty country where we're headin'," Jeb said with a slight chuckle cracking his voice. "You'll sure like the sights."

His attempts to calm her did little for her peace of mind. Platte Falls had the look of the dingy mining town which her father had described. Small wood-plank buildings separated by dirt streets and alleys. As they walked, the townspeople gawked as if they had never seen a woman from the East. Even the men at the Platte Falls Palace Saloon interrupted their drinking to come to the doorway and watch her pass. The farther she went, the worse she felt.

They stopped in front of the boarded-up sheriff's office, where horses were reined to a post.

"Are we leaving right away?" Besides her anger at John's absence, and thoughts of spite to keep him waiting, she wasn't anxious to leave town with these men for two days. "All I've had to eat for two days is some muffins with tea. Can't we have dinner first and leave in the morning? I'm quite exhausted from the trip."

"We'll have some grub—uh—supper on the way. When Mr. Rhodes sent us for you, he was awful mad he couldn't come get you hisself, and I know he wants to see you as soon as he can," Jeb said, tying her bags to the mare's saddle. "And he told us to make sure you were taken care of. And that's just what we're goin' to do. We're goin' to take good care of you. You can bet on that."

"Don't make that bet," said a voice behind them. Claire twisted around to see a tall, broad-shouldered man dressed in a green shirt so dark it appeared black. His pants and boots were the color of street dust. Tanned-hide leggings were laced tight up to the knees. A wide-brimmed black hat curled at the front, hiding his eyes, but the pistol holstered on his right hip and a long sheathed knife strapped to his belt were in plain view.

"Mrs. Rhodes," the stranger said in a threatening tone, "I think it best you come with me if you want to see your husband." He stepped onto the sidewalk directly in front of them.

Claire was appalled at his manner. "I beg your pardon?"

Jeb and Caleb pulled their coats away from their side arms.

"Who the hell are you, mister?" asked Jeb.

"Name's Cole. And the woman's coming with me."

"Excuse me, but—"

"I always did like to know who it was that I was gonna shoot," Jeb said as his grin widened.

Cole stared at the big burly man. "I never have."

"Jeb," Caleb mumbled, stepping back as if hit by lightning. "That's the Rainmaker fella."

Jeb's grin shrank. Slowly his hand moved away from his pistol and he stepped back as well. "Sorry, friend. Didn't know who you was. I don't want no trouble. No reason to use that Colt."

Cole stood stoically as he clasped his left hand over his right in front of his gunbelt.

Jeb continued backward from the sidewalk, separating himself from the stranger.

Claire shook her head in disbelief, bewildered by what was happening, not knowing who any of these men were. She did sense there was going to be a fight, and she was the prize.

Cole's head jerked up. A glint of steel came from an upstairs window across the street. Cole released his right hand, snatching his pistol and firing from the holster top. The shot went through the glass. A second later, a man crashed through the window in a dead man's fall to the street, a rifle buried under him.

The townspeople ran indoors and behind walls for protection.

Jeb drew and fired, splintering an awning pillar.

Cole threw himself to the side. Rolling to his feet, he shot twice at the big man. The bullets tore through Jeb's chest and out his back. He cringed with pain, then fell to the ground.

Claire screamed at the sight of blood squirting from the wounds, with Jeb's face seized in agony. The black-hatted gunman fired another shot into Jeb's chest.

Claire tried to scream again but had no breath to make a sound.

Caleb ran for the alley by the hotel while shooting over his shoulder. Cole flinched at the wild shots and swung aim at his next target.

Claire's mouth fell open in horror as she stared at the barrel of Cole's pistol, pointed directly at her. The chamber rolled as he pulled back the hammer. She saw his eyes as he yelled at her.

"Move!"

Claire sank to her knees.

Cole fired. Sparks and smoke came spitting out the muzzle. The stench of gunpowder filled the air. The piercing ring deafened her. She followed the exploding plume over her shoulder to see a red-misted halo floating over Caleb's head. The body dropped into a horse trough. The splash soaked two young boys hiding behind it.

Little Fred was already mounted and riding out of town. Cole glanced at Claire to see her crying, but unhurt. He ran across the street to a saddled Appaloosa, drawing a rifle from its scabbard.

He ran down the alley. At the back fence, he levered a cartridge into the Winchester's chamber and propped it between the planks at the fleeing rider. His left forefinger and thumb guided the muzzle as if it were an arrow. His aim steadied on Little Fred's head as he squeezed the trigger. The shot rang off. He squinted through the smoke to see the horse galloping over the horizon with its rider still mounted.

"Damn!"

He started back to the street.

Claire still knelt as Cole returned. He offered his hand to help her up, but she shrank away. He grabbed her arm and jerked her to her feet. The bonnet flew away with the yank.

"You'll come with me if you want to stay alive," he said, and began dragging her to the Appaloosa.

"Who are you? Why are you doing this?" she cried, shivering with fright.

Cole scabbarded the rifle. "We're getting out of town before someone else takes a shot at me."

"I demand an answer. I was almost killed. Why did you shoot those men? Who were those men? They promised to take me to my husband. Where are you taking me. Help! Hel—"

Cole put his hand over her mouth to stop the barrage of words, then tried to grab her waist. She slapped at his encroachment. He angrily slid his hands along the sides of her bust and found the seams of her sturdy corset.

Claire stood petrified. She raised her hand to slap him, but he lifted her up and threw her astride the saddled paint mare next to his gray horse. Claire straddled the horse, a position she wasn't accustomed to, still too stunned by this man's treatment of her to bother covering her exposed stockings.

Cole untied both horses and mounted the Appaloosa. He grabbed her horse's reins and galloped out of Platte Falls.

Claire hung on to the saddlehorn and her fallen curls flew up in the breeze. When the horses jumped the train tracks at the edge of town, she glanced back at the townspeople gathering around the dead men.

They rode until they were out of sight of the town. Then he slowed the horses to a trot and pulled up alongside of her.

"I'm sorry for the way I had to handle you

back there, Mrs. Rhodes." He pulled a canteen from the horn and offered her a drink. She tried not to look at him. "But there's one thing that you're going to have to learn out here. There a lot of people that want land, money, or the love of a pretty woman. Your husband has land and money, but he doesn't have his pretty woman. Not yet. So to some people you're worth a lot of land or a lot of money."

She looked at him, paying attention now to what he said.

"What if those gentlemen you murdered back there were truly trying to escort me to my husband and save me from men like you?" she choked out.

"Those men back there were likely going to take you and hold you for ransom. I recognized one of them, Caleb Hensley. He and his brother Carl robbed a few banks with the Corbin gang in Texas. He stole cattle, burned a few squatters' houses, and shot a few men in the back while doing it. He was no gentleman, and the others weren't churchgoers."

"You shot *him* in the back."

"And damn quick too. You don't give a man shooting at you a chance to get better aim, even if he is running from you."

"How do I know that you aren't going to kill me or hold me for ransom?"

"I guess you really don't," Cole answered as he reined in both horses. "You notice that nobody from town is coming after us? Gunfights and dead gunfighters are all part of living in a town such as Platte Falls. Now if I was going to kill you, or even worse, have my way with you then kill you, I could have done it by now."

Claire kept silent, not knowing if that was exactly what he intended to do.

Cole smirked and shook his head at the fright on her face. "As far as ransom, I was sent to bring you to your husband at his silver mine. And that's all I'm going to do." He pointed at the mountains ahead of them.

Her eyes followed, to gaze at the vast green hills. Then she noticed him looking at the descending sun.

"We only have an hour of light to make camp up there." He reached for the mare's reins, but Claire pulled them away.

"I know how to ride."

He grinned and spurred his horse. She did the same.

"I hope so. Tomorrow we ride through Danger Ridge."

Chapter Two

Little Fred held his horse's mane with one hand while covering the bloody hole in his left side with the other. Dusk allowed a flickering light from a nearby campfire to guide him through the mountain trees. He rode into camp, his hand losing its grip on the mane.

"Hold your fire, it's Little Fred," he shouted from the brush. Three men ran out from cover to catch the wounded man as he fell off his horse.

"What happened?" one asked.

An anguished groan was the answer.

"The boss said he wanted to see the first one of you that came back," another man said as he pointed to the main tent.

"He's hurt bad, Ben," the first one said.

Ben scowled at him. "You know that don't change nothing, Pete. The man said he wanted to see him."

They helped Little Fred hobble into the tent. He collapsed in a chair under the lantern.

The orange glow of a lit cigar emerged from the darkness of the far side of the tent. The outline of a man's face was illuminated by the radiance. His silk shirt and shimmering vest sparkled beneath his open black coat. He sat behind a table with a bottle of whiskey on it.

"He's hurt pretty bad," said Pete.

"Leave him there," a pitiless voice ordered. The others left the tent. "Where's the woman?"

Little Fred puffed out mumbled words, then grabbed the whiskey and took one long gulp from the bottle.

Carl Hensley raced into the tent and saw Little Fred drinking the liquor. He knocked the bottle away, shattering it on the ground. "What happened? Where's Caleb?" Hensley shouted as he snatched Little Fred's collar and lifted him.

"Dead, dead," was the answer. "They're both dead. Joe too. They're all dead."

"Who did it? There's no law in Platte Falls," the boss said from the darkness.

"I dunno. Some big fella. Looked like a raw-hider or maybe a buff hunter. He shot them all," Little Fred said as Hensley released and he fell on the chair. "*Rainmaker*, Caleb called him. Then he shot Joe in the hotel, quick as a snake-bite. Like he knew he was up there."

Carl's jaws tightened as he looked at the ground.

"What happened to Jeb and Caleb?" the boss asked.

"Don't know that either. I was runnin' then. But I heard some more shots. I knew they had to be dead because I couldn't hear 'em callin' no more. I just kept riding when I felt my side blowed open." The little man winced.

"Did you say the Rainmaker? You yellow son of a bitch." Hensley pulled his revolver. "You ran off and left them in a gunfight with the Rainmaker?"

"Carl!" the boss yelled, using a cane to stand. "Remember the men outside." Hensley holstered his weapon and took a step back in silent anger, running his hand through his red hair.

The boss limped over to the panting Little Fred and saw the blood-soaked dirt around the chair. "Ben! Pete! Come and take Little Fred and see to this wound," he called out. The two men came in and carried the small man out of the tent. The boss turned to Carl. "You sound like you know who this Rainmaker is."

"Yeah, I know him. From back in Texas. Son of a bitch almost killed me and Caleb. His name is Cole. He's a tough gun. He was an army scout, or so it was said when I knew him. I crossed up with him when we were chasing squatters from railroad land. When he left the territory, word was that he was being hunted as a deserter from the army."

"This man doesn't sound like a coward," the boss said, surprised.

"Story was that he was with Custer. Stayed with him all the way up to the Little Bighorn. Then he ran just before the battle. It was always said that he could smell trouble. Heard tell the army's been chasing him since. Was told a bounty was on his head too."

"You just remember the plan. We're only after the woman and the money. There's fifty thousand dollars traveling loose out there."

"That bastard killed my brother, left him dead in Platte Falls. Don't tell me to forget it," Carl raged.

The boss took a long puff on his cigar to let the tension ease. "You think he has the woman?"

"Cole wasn't the type to take women. But when you're a wanted man, I know you do things that you're not used to doin'."

"If he does have her, how can we get the money?"

"Well, there may be a way." Carl's scowl slackened. "If he does have her, it may be for ransom or reward, or it just may be to bring her to the mine."

Hensley's suggestion brought a concurring nod from the boss.

"What should we do?"

"I'd think a city woman would be trouble after

25

the first day. Cole would want to be rid of her as quick as he could. He could make it in two days, but there's only one known way to get to the mine from Platte Falls in two days," Carl said as he checked the chambers in his pistol.

"The north ridge? Danger Ridge?"

Carl nodded. "We'd have to ride near the river. It'd be the only way in the dark, but we could use torches. Cole couldn't be there before daybreak. We'll have to leave now to be able to set up for them. I'll take Hank, Lester, and the kid with me. The three of them can keep Cole busy while I concentrate on the woman."

"How so?"

Carl paused a moment before answering. "A Sharps .45–.70 gives you that. I could shoot her from a thousand yards and Cole couldn't do anything about it."

"Good," the boss said, taking another long puff of the cigar. "Just make sure that you get the job done. I'd just as soon not have that bitch showing up at the mine."

Carl Hensley nodded, making it clear he understood what he had been ordered to do. He left the tent and called the men to ride. Within moments their voices, the stretch of leather, and neighing horses were all that could be heard. The boss stayed in his tent until the sounds faded away.

When he came out, he viewed the semiconscious Little Fred lying on a bedroll by the fire. He stopped and stared at the flame. He had waited for this chance for a long time. Claire Rhodes would provide his one opportunity, and he had to take full advantage of it. He had hired the outlaw Hensley brothers and the other gunnies to help him put together a deal that would make him one of the richest men in the West. He couldn't allow some outsider like Cole to ruin it. He would just as soon have him dead, as well as the woman. He couldn't let her escape. He couldn't allow this chance to get by him.

A wheezing cough shook him from his trance. He unclenched his aching grip from the cane's handle and peered at Little Fred. Slowly he limped to stand over him.

The agonizing man blinked at his boss.

"I know you're hurting and need a doctor. But you'll just slow me down." The boss drew a double-shot Derringer from his pocket. "Nothing is going to slow me down. Nothing."

Chapter Three

The pop of a distant gunshot echoed through the hills. Claire heard the sound from a sheltering cave. A small fire lit up the cave from the darkness of night.

"What's that?" she asked.

"Sounds like partners parting ways," Cole replied, as he stirred beans and salt pork in a black kettle. Together with a tin coffeepot, the kettle hung suspended by a tripod over the campfire. "Not uncommon up here."

"Who could be out there? Do you think they're outlaws? Don't you think they will see the fire?"

"Do you want me to put it out?" Cole shook his head. "The shot came from the other side of the hills. The cave will keep the light down." He rose from his crouch and walked with some stiffness to the back of the cave, where he'd placed the saddles. He pulled out two plates and forks and a small canvas sack from the saddlebags and returned to the fire.

Claire couldn't stop twitching her legs and arms as she sat. The warmth of the flame was all she had to combat the brisk breeze sweeping into the cave. She rubbed her shoulders and arms with each gust. But her reactions weren't only from the night's chill.

Cole slopped some beans on a plate and reached in the sack for a biscuit. He offered the plate to her.

"No, thank you. I'm not hungry," she lied.

"More for me," he said, scooping the beans into his mouth with his fork.

She glared in disgust at his crude manners, then glanced at the outer darkness. "If those men in town were outlaws, how did they know about me? Who told them I was coming here?"

"Can't say."

"Well then, who sent you?"

"All I know is, a man who said he loved you very much."

"John? Why didn't he meet me at the train? Perhaps it's him out there searching for me now. He could be trying to resc—find me. Maybe he's already in Platte Falls wondering where I am."

"Then he'd be a damn fool. These hills are

dangerous enough during the light of day, but by night, they're deadly. It's nothing for a man to step right off a cliff or be thrown by his horse right into one of the canyons. I think any man like your husband would know better than to travel at night, not knowing exactly where it was he had to go."

Claire reluctantly agreed in silence. She wanted so much to be in her house or another safe haven, away from these circumstances she didn't understand and was unable to control. She felt sick from the uncertainty, the unfamiliarity of her surroundings, and her dependence on this man who she still didn't know if she could trust. All the warnings were coming true. Men shooting at one another seemed to be a way of life. It was the first time she had regretted coming west, but the delight this would give her gloating father spurred her to endure whatever hardships she would encounter. She had to rid herself of these ill feelings. Conversation seemed to be the only remedy.

"Have you ever been thrown off your horse, Mr. Cole?"

Cole wiped the plate clean with his biscuit and slopped more beans upon it, then tipped the pot, pouring the boiling java into his coffee tin. She hated the time it took him to answer. Finally he pushed the wide-brimmed hat back to reveal his grin-cracked face. "More times than my body likes to remember."

She smiled in reflex at the sight of him smiling. The fire's glow lit up his sky-blue eyes from his reddened face. His stubble appeared as a light shadow over his scar-lined cheeks. At last she sensed she was talking to another human being.

"What's its name?" she asked, just to keep talking.

"Name? Whose name?"

"The name of your horse?"

"Name a horse?" The smile was gone.

"Yes. I thought that all cowboys out here in the West gave pet names to their horses. Something about being the only companions that they have in the wilderness. I read it in a book."

Cole paused again, finishing his latest mouthful, which seemed to give him enough time to civilize his answer.

"Is that a fact?" he mocked. "Well, that may be what 'cowboys' do, although I doubt it. I can't say what you've been reading, Mrs. Rhodes, but out here you try not to get fond of too many things, because most times you end up losing whatever it is. Whether it's your saddle, or some other property, or maybe even your horse." He turned his head toward the cave opening, puffed out his cheeks, and spat a piece of pork gristle. "And my horse is no pet, and I'm no drover."

His snide tone didn't deter her. "Yes, I'd read that it is quite dangerous here. The events in Platte Falls showed the truth of that." She looked into the fire, then back at him. "Doesn't it bother you that you killed those people?"

His eyes stared back at her. "There are a lot of good folk here. But good folk attract the bad ones. Just as snakes are found in a barn. Killing men like them back there is just like killing snakes." He took another mouthful of beans. "I never enjoyed killing a man, but you get used to it."

"I had read that too about men in the West."

"Well, I'm glad to see there's some truth to whatever you're reading," he said, then slurped the steaming coffee. "That being the case, Mrs. Rhodes, if you ask me, I think it a foolish idea of your husband's, bringing a woman of your upbringing here. There's no life for a lady at a silver mine." He finished the last bite of beans on his plate.

"You sound just like my father, Mr. Cole." She grinned. "He didn't think much of me coming here either."

"Sounds like a smart fellow, your father." He splashed the plate with water from his canteen to clean it.

"My father is a very smart man. And a very powerful one. His name is Jacob Thorsberg. Maybe you have heard of him. He owns one of the largest shipbuilding companies in Baltimore . . . in the entire country for that matter. It was impossible to convince him that I should come out here and live with John at his mine. Nevertheless, I told him that if I was the wife of a silver mine owner in the mountains of Colorado, I should be there at his side."

Cole pulled a pouch from his pocket, tapped some of the contents on a paper, and rolled a cigarette. "So, why did Mr. Rhodes come all the way out here with your father being so rich and powerful? Prospecting is a pretty risky business at best." He lit the cigarette with a coal-tipped branch, then stoked the fire with it. The scent of the igniting cedar helped put her at ease.

"My father is the reason John left Baltimore to come here. At first the two of them were almost like father and son. John worked for him, starting as one of the supply buyers for ship materials. Then, in a matter of months, John was Daddy's assistant in the manufacturing operations. That's when I met him." She paused a moment and pointed her nose toward the kettle. "That does smell good now. For some reason my appetite has returned. May I have some?"

Cole slowly rose and walked toward the saddlebags. "Then did you get married?"

"Oh, that wasn't for some time. John and I did see each other regularly at my father's office, then we courted for almost two years before my parents would consent for us to be married; my father wanted me to continue at Smith College, but I wanted to be Mrs. John Rhodes, so I left after my second year. Mother insisted I be twenty-three before I wed. That was her age when she married my father. John and I married two years ago and shortly thereafter, things seemed to turn for the worse." She paused. "John and Daddy began to be at odds with each other, mostly it seemed over money matters. It turned so bitter that Daddy began accusing John of marrying me for my family's money. But I told him he was wrong. John loves me. My father is a stubborn man, Mr. Cole. And he can be a harsh man too."

Cole seemed uncomfortable with her anguish. "Here, eat some of this," he said hurriedly, while slopping beans and pork onto the plate with the remaining biscuit. "I didn't mean to upset you, Mrs.—"

"No, that's not your fault, Mr. Cole." She took the plate from him and began to move the beans on the plate as she gathered her thoughts. "You have a right to know who it is you're traveling with, and I have to say that I feel somewhat more comfortable speaking about it."

He poured her a tin full of coffee and placed it on the ground beside her, then drank his own.

"A little over a year ago, John met a man named Hoyt Larsen, who told him about the western territories, and the fact that there was an abundance of gold and silver being found here. Well, John saw huge fortunes to be made in the mining of these minerals, and convinced me that this was his chance to make it on his own, away from my father's harassment."

"Harassment?"

"Oh yes. Even though he is my father and I love him very much, he can be quite brutal in his criticism. And he hounded John about his mistakes in the business and . . ." She hesitated. "I apologize for boring you with my family matters.

"Oh, no," he muttered, trying to sound interested but not encouraging her to continue. "You have any children?" he asked, in an obvious effort to change the subject.

She shook her head.

He casually pointed at her. "That's a pretty sparkler you got there."

She touched her brooch, then smiled at him. "Thank you. It's been in my family for four generations. My mother gave it to me when I married John." Suddenly she sniffed the air. "That tobacco has the most bizarre aroma. It's almost intoxicating."

"That is a fact. Doesn't have the bite of whiskey either. It's not store-bought, though. I traded with a Kiowa for it. No telling where he got it."

The small diversion helped her to relax. Although odd, the confession she was giving this stranger had made her feel better, even if he didn't seem to want to hear it.

"You see, shortly after we were wed, John became distant. So much so that I began to sense that he blamed me for his arguments with my father. He also became afflicted . . ." She hesitated again. "He has trouble walking. It made him bitter at the world. That's why he was so eager to set out on his own when the chance came. I agonized over whether to go, but John insisted I shouldn't; one of the few things my parents and he agreed on. So he left. And now, a year later, I decided to leave Baltimore to join him here. So here I am, together with my things and my endowment." She ate the beans.

"Endowment?"

She nodded, then swallowed. "Funds."

"You mean money?" Cole flicked his cigarette into the flames. He swigged down the remains of his coffee.

"Yes," she answered, while dipping her fork into the beans. "Enough to start a new life for the both of us."

"You brought it with you—out here?"

Claire nodded, confused as to why he appeared upset.

"Oh lord," he lamented. "Who knows this?"

"John. He had asked that I send it first by Wells-Fargo, but I decided to surprise him by coming at the same time. I telegrammed that I would be traveling with it as a safeguard."

Cole shook his head. "Everyone west of the Great Divide must know about this. No wonder Hensley and the others were waiting for you in Platte Falls. Where is this money?"

"I had to leave it at the train station because those men said they couldn't bring it to the mine," she answered, starting to recognize how foolish she seemed. "Mr. Cole, I know what you must be thinking, but I'm perfectly capable of handling my affairs. You sound just as my father did. That's why I had to withdraw the money without his consent, because he'd never have let me come here with it."

"Yeah, well, sounds like another thing him and I see the same way." He pulled out his revolver and opened the chambergate. "All of a sudden, I have a real bad feeling about tomorrow's ride. The last time I had a feeling this bad, I was with—" He paused. "Well, never mind." He stared blankly at the revolver. "It's time we got some sleep. Tomorrow will be a full day's ride."

When she finished her last portion of beans, he took the plate and started to clean it. Then he picked up both bedrolls and laid one on each side of the fire. She stood and stared at him in bewilderment, then folded her arms.

"I don't intend to sleep on the ground."

"It's a long stroll back to the Platte Falls Palace," he said, while taking off his leggings.

"But I can't sleep on the ground." She looked at her surroundings. "Well, certainly not in this dress."

Cole peered up at her, then slowly rose to his feet and picked up his hat and bedroll. He left the cave to her.

She removed her brooch and started to remove her clothes, then thought better of it. She had no idea what effect a near naked woman would have on this western man. Reluctantly, she sank down to the bedroll and threw the blanket over herself. After what seemed like hours, she had unfastened the blue taffeta dress and unlaced the tightly strung corset. All the while she kept a watchful eye on the darkness outside the cave. After slipping her clothes off, she folded them as best she could and pulled the blanket up to her chin. "Goodnight, Mr. Cole."

There was no reply.

Chapter Four

A rustling sound broke the still of the morning. Claire blinked the short night's sleep from her eyes to focus on the movement of her taffeta dress. She quickly rolled over to find herself still alone in the cave. The night's fire was a pile of smoldering embers. A chirp drew her eyes back to her moving dress, and a moment later a dark-furred animal with a long white stripe emerged from the hem.

Claire squealed as she grabbed the dress and shook out the polecat, then ran from the cave. She immediately saw the shirtless Cole saddling the horses. He had turned with the shriek, then chuckled, watching the varmint walk off into the woods.

"Morning, Mrs. Rhodes," he said, continuing to saddle the horses.

Claire realized she was wearing only her camisole and pantaloons. She quickly raised the dress to shield her body from him and ran back into the cave. The embarrassment of being seen nearly naked was shortly overcome by her curiosity. She peeked around the cave to spy on him without his notice. His hair flowed back over his ears onto his neck. His broad shoulders rippled while he tugged the cinch. His chest and stomach were rigid but seemed dwarfed by the large, muscle-creased arms. The pants were tight to his waist as if part of his skin, and the leggings around his boots bulged at the top like an hourglass. His physique reminded her of the sculptures she'd seen in New York museums.

He spotted her head poking out and she quickly ducked back.

"We'll be leaving soon. Clouds look like a storm coming and I want to be past Danger Ridge before it hits," he called out.

"I would like to freshen before breakfast if you don't mind."

"No breakfast this morning. Can't chance the smoke being seen."

"You weren't worried about that last night," she said, poking her head fully into his view.

"It's easier to see black smoke in the light of day."

She realized his logic, but still didn't appreciate it; she couldn't remember a day of her life without breakfast.

"Then you'll at least let me wash myself."

"Go ahead. There's a creek just down the side there."

She saw the creek at the bottom of the hill. She raised the dress around her again and crept out of the cave, ever watchful of his eyes, which were still turned away to the horses.

She carefully stepped on the leaves and stones that covered the side of what she could now see was a steep incline. She crouched as she descended and gained confidence with every step. A familiar sound made her look behind her. It was the skunk.

She squealed again and lost her balance. Her left foot flew out from under her. Tumbling down the slope, rolling in the leaves and mud, she finally landed facedown in the creek.

She peered up to see Cole at the edge of the hill with his pistol drawn. When she saw him, he uncocked the pistol with a look of disgust. "I see you found it."

Claire rose from the creek bed. Mud covered her arms and legs but the front of her camisole and pantaloons were rinsed clear of it. She stopped shaking the mud off her hands long enough to notice that the transparent clinging cloth was showing the contour of her breasts. She crossed her arms in front of them only to see the dark spot below her waist showing through her pantaloons. She crouched and looked up at Cole, but he had left from sight. Thoroughly humiliated, she wanted to cry, but growled in frustration instead.

A short time later she came up the hill, holding the saturated dress to cloak her body. Cole sat fully dressed on a rock near the horses. She sneered at his gaze as she reentered the cave. "I can't travel like this and I haven't any other clothes. I'll have to hang them to dry."

"Can't wait that long. Looks like that storm is closing in fast and I don't want to get caught up in it."

"Well, I can't show up to my husband naked!"

"I put some of my clothes in there. You should find them. I know they're man's things, but they'll do until we get there."

She found the dry clothes and held them up against her. Although dismayed with the thought of wearing men's clothes, she didn't have any alternative.

She pulled the camisole from her shoulders and put on the stiff cotton shirt. After a deep breath, she glanced outside, then quickly removed her pantaloons and stepped into the pants. She hopped to get her feet through the legs. The waist of the pants stopped just under her chest. She put her brooch in a pocket and took another deep breath. Little time passed before she emerged wearing the four-sizes-too-big white shirt and trousers with a large knot at the waist. She still wore her brown suede shoes, but without stockings. She held the dripping undergarments as she walked to the paint mare.

"Where shall I pack these?" she asked.

"Leave 'em."

"I shall not! These are my clothes. I won't have them lying about for someone to come and admire as they please. Not to mention for any of these animals to tear apart."

"Well, I wouldn't worry much about someone finding them out here," he said, mounting the Appaloosa. "Besides, they'll dry quicker if you leave 'em lay out. They'll just smell if you roll them in the bedroll."

She hated the thought of leaving her beautiful dress.

"You can come back later and get them in a few days. If need be, I'll come after them for you."

She looked up at him, reasoning out his offer.

"I promise."

She again found herself agreeing with him; a thought that made her feel like a child. She stretched the undergarments out on a large boulder and walked over to the paint. She stopped and slowly gave Cole a piercing stare.

Now Cole looked bewildered as to why she delayed mounting the horse, until he saw her open palm pointing at the stirrup.

"Is it broke?"

She shook her head.

He rolled his eyes, took a breath, dismounted, and walked up behind her. She didn't know what she enjoyed more; the triumph of forcing him to show his gentlemanly side, or the firm feel of his hands on her hips as he lifted her onto the horse.

Two hours in the saddle wore into Claire's enthusiasm to continue as much as into her aching backside. She changed positions constantly to revive her tingling joints, all the while following Cole's single-file lead up the endless tree-lined trail.

He pulled up upon reaching a clearing and she took advantage of the break in routine to come up alongside. "What is it?"

He spoke softly. "Up there. Two riders, and they look to be Mex. Don't see much of their kind up here. Those that I've seen are mostly on the run from the law, or will soon have reason to be."

She strained to see the two figures approaching. One was an older man with a distinguished gray beard. He wore a flat-brimmed black hat, flaming red shirt, and light-colored chaps. The other appeared to be a boy, just younger than herself. His hat was similar, but the dust-covered shirt seemed white under his brown vest coat. As they neared, Cole whispered, "Don't do or say anything."

"*Buenos días, Ustedes. Mi nombre es Ramiro Fuentes y este es mi hijo, Miguel. Andamos a mi hijo, Casimiro,*" the older man said. Cole's face remained stern, his right hand poised inches away from his holster.

"Mr. Cole—"

"Hush."

"¿Nos puede ayudar?" the older man inquired.

Cole made no attempt to reply.

"El se fue' de la casa en Santa Fe, hace seis semanas por razónes de negocios. Le agradeciera cualquier información."

Claire sensed tension at Cole's silence. The Mexicans didn't seem a threat and their expressions showed the sincerity of trying to communicate. She sensed there would be trouble and that she could stop it from happening. "I know what—"

"If they move their hands, you jump off that horse and keep your head down."

"Yo no hablo Inglés," the older man said. *"¿Usted habla español?"* He looked confused. *"Yo le pago por su ayuda."* He turned to the young man. *"Miguel, enseñales el dinero."* The young man reached inside his vest coat.

Cole's hand slid back to his holster and gripped the Colt.

"No es necesario!" Claire shouted.

Cole froze at the sound of her voice. Slowly, his dropjawed face turned to her.

She smiled.

Both Mexicans looked just as shocked at her announcement, as Miguel withdrew a weighted pouch from his coat.

"No, Señor," she said. *"No hemos visto a tu hijo. No hemos visto a nadie hoy."*

"You talk Mex?" Cole asked.

"The language is Spanish. And yes, I speak it fluently," she muttered. *"Hay un pueblo que se llama Platte Falls. A el oeste de aquí. Tal vez lo encuentré allí."*

"Muchas gracias, Señora," the older man said graciously as he tipped his hat. Both men ambled their horses past her and Cole.

"De nada. Ojalá lo encuentre," she answered as the two rode away.

"Why didn't you tell me you talked Mex? You could have got us both killed," Cole barked as he tucked the Colt in his holster.

"I tried. But you wouldn't let me say a word. I am also fluent in French and Dutch. Would you like to hear?"

"What did you tell them? How did you get them to leave?"

"They were looking for the older gentleman's son. I just told them that we hadn't seen anyone and suggested they go to Platte Falls and look for him there."

He shook his head as he nudged the Appaloosa.

"Ladies are taught more than proper posture at Smith College. There are many things about me you don't know, Mr. Cole."

"I am sure of that, Mrs. Rhodes." His tone showed his irritation with her.

She brought the paint next to him. "How much farther to the mine?"

"I can't tell you for sure."

"I beg your pardon. I didn't hear you clearly.

46

It sounded like you said that you didn't know."

"You heard right."

Claire took a deep breath. "Then how could you bring me all the way out here if you didn't know where you were going?"

Cole turned to her with a scowl she recognized from the last time she'd nagged him. "We're going to meet up with a friend of mine. He has a shack on the other side of Danger Ridge."

"There's that place again. Just where is this Danger Ridge, and what is so dangerous about it?"

"It's the quickest way to get from here to there. We save three days' riding. There's no words I know that describe it good enough. There's just some things that their name fits. This place is one of them. We'll be there soon enough."

Claire thought about what he'd said. There was another name about which she wanted to know more. "Is that why that man, Caleb, called you the Rainmaker? Are you like the Indians I've heard of in these western expositions that dance and chant to make it rain?" Cole chuckled again just as he had the night before. She liked him much better when he laughed.

"No. That was what my ma had people call me when I was little."

"Oh. Well, what does she call you now?"

His expression turned somber before he replied. "She passed on back in sixty-one."

Claire felt a fool for inquiring. "I'm sorry. I didn't mean—"

"Don't be. It was a long time back. Consumption took her that winter. I don't think about it much now." He paused for a moment. "Clay," he said, staring straight ahead. "She would call me Clay."

The path opened to a wide grassed expanse.

"Who are you, Clay Cole?" she asked, watching his face for the answer. Moments went by before he looked to her.

"How you mean?"

"Well, how old are you? Where are you from?" She paused before asking, "Is there a lady in your life?"

"You often ask that of people you hardly know?"

"Only the ones that are responsible for my safety, and those I travel with to the most remote areas of the wilderness. And, I might add, those who have seen me in only . . ." She hesitated, unsure of whether her teasing might further embarrass herself or maybe even him. "Well, let us say few are as familiar with me as I have found you to be on this trip."

"That wasn't my doing."

"No, I have to say that if I weren't quite so clumsy . . ." She stopped again for the same reason. "Well, if you aren't going to tell me about yourself, then tell me about this other man that I'll soon be at the mercy of."

"Jenks? Well, he's just a man. Nothing much

about him. Can be crotchety at times, but living up here by yourself can make you that way."

"Then he's a hermit?"

"Not in the usual sense, but you could say that."

"Then how did you come to know him if he lives up here by himself? Were you both hermits?"

"Met him back when I was a trooper. He was with a scout name of Hickok that was working for the Seventh Cavalry years back. I met up with him then."

"So, you were a soldier for General Custer."

"Yeah." He nodded. "But he'd been busted down to colonel then. Hated it too. He always thought of himself as a general, even before they made him one in the States War. Anyway, I learned fairly quick that it paid more being a scout than soldiering. So when my two-year hitch was over, I joined up with Jenks after he and Hickok left the Seventh in sixty-seven. Rode with them till Hickok wanted to be a lawman and Jenks didn't. So the two of us were together for a couple of summers working for the army killing buffalo. But you get tired of killing after a long time doing it, especially when you're just doing it to be killing, even if it is just animals."

Claire sensed something in his voice that she hadn't heard before, but it was gone as quickly as it came.

"So Jenks thought about mining. He liked being alone. He didn't take to people much, but I never had the patience for mining. We split up, let's see . . . been five years now."

"This Jenks person sounds like Henry Thoreau."

"Don't know of him. Is he kin to you?"

She giggled. "No. But he did have a friend named Ralph Emerson that I much admired. He wrote about the benefits of self-reliance—a trait I feel defines a person's qualities." Her comment sparked her own curiosity. "Then what did you do?"

"Well, I went back to scouting. Say, you do ask a lot of questions of people, Mrs. Rhodes. You must be one of them reporters or something back East. Are you?"

"No." She smirked. "I just feel better knowing certain things about people. And please, call me Claire."

"Okay, Claire."

His smile was the one thing which she had come to welcome.

He slowed his horse. "There it is. Danger Ridge."

Claire turned to gaze at what was before them. They had crested the expanse, and with every step of the horses, the jagged peak of the massive cragged escarpment appeared to climb higher in the sky.

"This is as high as we'll ever be, so take a good look."

They both pulled up to admire what they saw. Hills and valleys in the distance, covered with the green of fir, pine, and spruce that rose and fell like waves in the sea. Farther away were the snowcapped mountaintops, piercing through the clouds in long rows stretching to the horizon.

"It's beautiful. There's so much, I don't think one can see enough to see it all," she said, still in awe of the view.

"It is a sight. Took my breath first time I came up here. Those thinking that the West begins at the Mississippi must never have thought they'd see this."

He held his horse, watching Claire moving her head from side to side, reviewing what she had seen. He gently spurred the Appaloosa to start down the hill, to cross the ridge. The paint followed behind without a command from Claire.

The expanse gave way to a narrow passage. She continued to look up at the top of the ridge as they descended. They neared the small pass at the base, but she kept looking at clouds crawling over the rocky apex, until her eyes teared from staring so long. When she looked down to wipe them, she found herself on a very confined ledge with fallen rocks to her right and a sloping wooded precipice below to her left.

"What's down there? I can't see what's on the bottom," she said, stretching to peek through the firs and spruce below, careful not to lose her grip on the horn.

"Ravine."

"How far down is it?"

"Well, that's another thing you could say I don't know for sure. Nobody's heard back from those that made the trip."

She bit her lip to keep from answering his remark. A firm kick to the mare's flanks closed the distance to the Appaloosa.

Cole reined in suddenly as his mount threw its head up and tried to back away.

"What's wrong? Why don't we go on?"

"I can't say, but I don't like being stopped here," he answered quietly, slowly looking around. "There it is. That's the reason." He pointed to the ground, where there was a large depression in the soft mud between the rocks. "Grizzly. That's why they're nervous. And judging by the size of that paw, it's an adult male, seven or eight feet and better than a thousand pounds of him."

Claire's eyes fixed on the print as the paint grew jittery.

"If he's close by, he's not going to care for us being here." Cole drew the Winchester from the scabbard under his left knee and levered a round into the chamber.

"I don't see anything. How would it even know we're here?"

"Scent," Cole said as he turned to her. "He can smell you."

Claire dipped her head to the shirt and sniffed. "It can't be me. It must be these clothes."

The paint whinnied and reared up. Claire clutched the reins and dug in her heels to stay on.

The paint's head exploded. Blood splattered in the air. Claire fell off the collapsing animal and down the slope.

Chapter Five

Cole dove from the bolting Appaloosa. Bullets flew past him. When he hit the ground, he glanced up to see a drifting plume of gray smoke coming from far up the ridge. Dust popped into the air from lead pelting the ground. He quickly crawled to the cover of a large boulder and looked back at the dead paint, but there was no sign of Claire. If she was still alive, she owed her life to her nervous horse, who jumped in the path of a bullet meant for her.

The gunfire from above continued, shattering bits of rock from the boulder. The shots sounded near, too near to be coming from where he saw the smoke. He quickly poked his head around the protective stone to look again. A man stood in the high rocks and seemed to be reloading a long-barreled rifle. The shape of it was familiar. No carbine could reach him where he stood.

A bullet ricocheted off the boulder, and chips stung Cole's face. He rolled back and dug out the large fragments that were embedded in his bleeding cheek and jaw.

The shots seemed to have a timed pattern. First one, then another, then another, all from different directions. He stuck out the Winchester and blindly fired twice to keep whoever it was from advancing on him. The peppering assault continued. They weren't trying to hit him now, they wanted to keep him pinned down.

He fired twice more, then took another quick look in time to see the man on the rocks aiming his weapon.

Claire slowly shook her head as she regained consciousness. She felt a throbbing pain in her ankle. She reached down and rubbed it and looked back up through the trees, where it sounded as if a battle was being waged. Then she remembered what had happened and realized that she was on the edge of the bluff. Slowly, she peered over the cliff to view the distant ravine below. She closed her eyes and lay back to ease the pain from her injury, all the time listening to the gunshots.

Where was Cole? Was he killed? Maybe he

was one of those shooting? Thoughts flew through her mind as she kept fighting the pain.

Through her concentration, she heard another sound. The sound of breathing, very heavy breathing. She knew then she wasn't alone on that bluff.

She gradually opened her eyes and looked over her shoulder to find a huge animal, twenty feet up the slope, staring right at her. It had thick reddish-brown fur and a black nose twitching at the end of its foot-long muzzle. Standing as tall as a horse at the shoulder, this thing matched the size of a carriage. It couldn't be a bear; bears weren't this big. This had to be some other creature. Her heart raced. She couldn't breathe.

The animal jerked its head in reaction to the distant gunfire. Claire attempted to move away but the motion drew the beast's attention to her. A rock between them flew apart, spraying dust, clouding the air. A loud whirring passed. Claire thought she'd been rescued, but as the dust quickly thinned, her relief turned to terror when she saw the animal's gaping mouth open, exposing dagger-like teeth and bellowing a deafening roar. She fell back and rolled nearer the edge. The giant monster came closer.

Cole recognized the thunderous blast of a Sharps, but the shot didn't come near him. He was still crouched behind the boulder and now was the time to get out, while the Sharps single-shot rifle was being reloaded.

He rose from behind the shielding boulder, sighting the Winchester on the first movement he saw: one of the attackers aiming a Henry rifle right at him. Both men shot, but only Cole's bullet found its mark, piercing the attacker's throat, dropping him behind the rocks.

Cole stroked the lever and looked for his next target. A young kid, not more than eighteen, came from cover raising a rifle. Cole fired quickly, winging the kid's right shoulder, making him drop the rifle in front of him. Cole levered and fired again, striking the kid's gut. Blood splattered the rocks behind the boy, but he continued to reach for the weapon, which lay just out of his grasp. Cole levered, the spent shell ejecting over his shoulder, and fired once more, mercifully ending the young man's life with a slug between the eyes.

Dust sprayed up from the boulder top. The whir of a spinning bullet passed by his ear. Cole fired into the cloud and waited for a cry. He heard nothing. As the screening dirt blew away, the figure of a man took shape. It was a man with a rifle aimed at him. Cole sank behind the boulder. A shot cracked the air.

He threw his hat out in the clear. The dirt popped up around it. Cole rose and fired at the lingering gunsmoke, but no one was there.

He watched through the gunsights for the third shooter, who hadn't revealed himself. His aim was steadied on the rocks, where he was sure the man hid. He drew a bead on a white sweat-banded Stetson edging up from cover. Cole squeezed off the round. The Stetson instantly turned red and another Henry rifle fell out from the rocks. With three men down, Cole planned the path to the lone gunman in the high rocks.

He sneaked up the steepening incline, angling away from the sniper's view, which still seemed fixed on something down below. There was only one way to get a shot. He would sweep around him and catch him by surprise, so the deadly long range of the Sharps wouldn't be useful.

With every step, Cole came closer, until falling stones drew the gunman's attention. Cole dropped into the cradling shelter of the rocks just as the lead whirred over his head. He wasn't within range to hit the man, but this would be the only chance to advance, while the Sharps was being reloaded.

Firing as fast as he could pump the repeater's lever, Cole climbed from the rocks and charged the gunman. Bullets flew wild, well in front of his target, but his aim narrowed in with every stride he took.

The gunman ceased his reloading and ran from his nest like a spooked quail. Now Cole had a clear shot. Although stretching the range of a carbine, he might be able to arc up enough to compensate. He stopped running and shouldered the Winchester, head steady, eyes locked on the quarry.

A howling call crept into his ear; a sound that broke his concentration when he recognized it. The call came again and his attention turned toward it. It came from the bluff. He glanced at the escaping sniper, then began moving down the ridge, slowly at first, then gaining speed, jumping from one boulder to another as the call became a voice, a howling, screaming voice.

"Clay!"

Claire was alive, but hearing the panic in every scream, he knew only moments separated her from death.

"Clay!"

He landed on the ledge in mid stride and chased the screams down the slope. Skidding on small pebbles, he fell on his back and slid down through the tall pines. Momentum propelled him with such force, he rolled on his side to gain control of his balance until he came to his feet at end of the trees.

He waved away the flying dust to see the largest grizzly bear he'd ever seen hovering on the edge of the cliff. A second later, it spotted him and stood defensively on its hind legs, growling, ears back.

The enormity of the charging bear blocked all else from view. Cole got the carbine as far as his waist before the bear knocked it away with one swipe. His hands filled with hide when the bear lunged at his legs. The crushing jaws glanced off his calves. The thick leggings were all that stopped the claws from ripping into flesh, but the grizzly reared, lifting Cole back and slamming his shoulders against the trunk of a pine.

Cole grabbed a small log to use as a club. The frothing snout opened to crush his throat, but he instinctively thrust the log at the teeth, jamming it at the back of the killer's jaws. The animal shook its head to free the choking object, but Cole pushed harder, knowing death followed the moment he failed to keep it there.

The forepaws pinned his right arm to his side, keeping his hand away from his pistol and knife. Breath wheezed through his gritted teeth while his arms were pressed further into his collapsing ribs. Strength faded from his left arm, allowing the points of the canines to brush against his neck. The light of day blinked dimmer.

All he sensed was the stench of the killer's breath huffing into his face, the wiping of its slobbered nose across his brow. In a panicked rage, Cole arched his neck to escape the fangs and butted his forehead against the nose. The pressure stopped.

The bear reared its head. The wooden club came loose. Cole took a large sucking breath during the grizzly's tormented sneeze. Cole pounded the twitching nose with the club, ramming it into the soft tissue. The injured animal released its death grip.

Cole dropped to his knees. The bear retreated

into the trees, shaking its head and sneezing.

Cole fell on his face, inhaling life back into his lungs.

"Clay!"

The cry came from the cliff. Driving himself to crawl to the edge, he saw Claire suspended with one hand clutching a slender branch of a small bush protruding from the escarpment. Her terrified eyes stared into his. She tried to pull herself up, but the bush began to come free from the rocky crevice. Cole threw his right arm over the edge to grab her wrist.

The branch snapped.

Chapter Six

The jolt from snatching Claire's arm dragged Cole over the cliff's edge. He snagged the exposed roots of the protruding bush with his bloody left hand. Their fall stopped, they dangled on the side of the bottomless ravine. Cole looked down at Claire's face, her mouth wide open, grunting, crying, screaming. Her eyes peeking from the corners to look down.

"Look—at—me!"

Her eyes locked on to his. He turned to look at the snarled roots as they slipped through his bloody fingers. He tightened his escaping grasp, realizing the weight would soon pull out the bush.

"Climb up on me," he shouted, bracing his left

foot against the rocks, then rolled his head back. He concentrated, blocking the pain. His arms ached. All the agony in his entire body was released through a grunting yell, increasing with every strained contraction of the muscles in his right arm.

The heel of Claire's shoe stabbing his right hip stopped the cry. He pulled her up until he felt the weight decreasing; she had reached the edge. She kicked his face as she tried to find footing. He grabbed her foot and put it on his shoulder then put his hand firmly on her backside.

She stiffened.

He shoved her higher. Dust and pebbles rained down on his face. She jumped off of him and pulled herself to safety.

Spitting the blood from his lips, he felt the delicate ends of the extracted roots. He unsheathed his long Bowie knife and jabbed it into a small crevice as the bush came free. Using both hands, he pulled against the handle of the sturdy blade and latched onto the edge of the rocky cliff. With one heaving yank he pulled his torso over the edge. Taking a few reviving breaths, he scooted his body to solid ground.

"You all right?" he huffed between gulps of air.

Claire nodded, her chin quivering.

"I'm not." He held his tingling left hand while looking at her.

"You saved my life," she said, her voice cracked.

He nodded. "You know now why it's called Danger Ridge?" His tone didn't allow any thought of accepting her gratitude. He continued rubbing the feeling back into his bloody hand.

She grabbed his hand and wrapped the long ends of her shirt around it to stop the bleeding. "I owe you my life," she repeated, so as to get a response.

"I know that. I almost made you lose it too. I should've known somebody would try something in this place. Damn near got us both killed three times."

Claire looked around. "What happened?"

"Don't know for sure. Somebody was trying to stop us from passing."

"Where are they?"

"Three are dead. The last one cleared out. Looked familiar, but I can't be sure."

"Why did they attack us? Were they trying to kill you?"

Cole paused. "One of us. That's for sure. Must have had a good reason, too. Just how much money did you bring with you, Mrs. Rhodes?"

She stared at the trees, then looked him in the eye. She didn't want to tell him, but he had just saved her life. She had to be honest with him. "Fifty thousand dollars in gold certificates."

Cole stopped breathing. He turned his head to the dirt and nodded. "That's a damn good reason." He looked back at her. "We can count on more of their type along the way."

"Did you kill that animal too?" she asked while tearing a long strip of cloth from the shirttail to bandage his wound.

"No. But I did give him a pain that he's never known."

A distant flash on the horizon brought his attention to a new problem. He saw the approaching dark blue clouds stretched over the sky like a huge awning. "Looks like we're going to be wet too," he said, resheathing the knife.

He retrieved his hat and rifle and walked back to her. She was still sitting motionless, as if in a trance. He offered his bandaged hand and she looked up at him. "Feels a little better now." She took his hand and he gently helped her up. "Let's get going. Rain looks like it's over Platte Falls now. We might make Jenks's cabin before it gets here and covers up the light."

Lightning lit up Platte Falls like the noon sun, then darkness reclaimed the night. Rain came down in sheets, turning rooftops into waterfalls. Streets were rushing streams from the mountain's runoff. The townspeople were all inside, having locked every window and door to keep out the storm's fury.

The lone light from the Platte Falls Palace was all that guided twelve riders to shelter. The lead rider took notice of three coffins stacked in a buckboard as they passed by the vacant sheriff's office. The riders stopped in front of the saloon.

"Column, dismount."

The batwing doors slowly opened and the caped leader walked into the silent saloon. A single chandelier lit the cavernous room. A bartender stacked chairs in the center. A man with a rolled-up pantleg who looked to be in a stupor sat at a table near the window.

The leader's hat had an emblem of crossed swords. He shook the water from his cape and threw it backward to reveal his uniform. Gold oak leaves adorned his shoulders. His neatly trimmed black beard framed a stern face as he walked toward the bar. He was met there by the scurrying bartender.

"Evening, Major," greeted the bartender. "What can I get you?"

"I need food and a night's quarters for myself and my men. I can pay you in government greenbacks," the officer said coldly as other cavalrymen filed inside.

"Well, the cook shut down the kitchen when the storm hit. Most people lock in when it gets like this."

The major scowled.

"But I'm sure I can fix up something for you and your men."

The expression didn't change.

"And as far as rooms for the night, well, all eight are filled with Rosie's girls. But you can bunk out here if you like."

A slow turn of the major's head to the floor told the bartender what he'd forgotten. "Of course, you can have my room in back, sir. I can stay out here."

The major nodded. "Very accommodating of you."

The bartender smiled in relief. "Would you and the men care for anything to drink while I cook your supper, sir?"

The major shook his head. "This branch of the army doesn't drink."

The bartender's smile disappeared. "Well, I guess I'll see what I can find," he said as he moved around the bar.

The major spoke, interrupting the bartender's walk. "When we rode in, I saw three pine boxes left outside."

"Oh, them's just some strangers got shot in a fight yesterday."

"Doesn't the sheriff around here see to the burial of those people rather than leaving them in the rain?"

"Oh, we ain't got a sheriff. Can't keep one long enough before they see they can make more money mining. Or they get shot dead. Those are the main two causes."

"Then who shot those men?"

"Ole Charley over there said two boys saw some other stranger gun them all down. Shot one of them fellows out of a window before that fellow could get a shot off. Just the one man did in all three of them. Hey, Charley."

The drunken man slowly raised his wobbling head.

"The major wants to know who those boys said it was that gunned down them three yesterday."

"Rain—Rainma—Rainmaker," the drunk stuttered.

The major's head shot up. The chatter from the men turned to a muddle of shouts, until the officer's raised hand brought them to silence. "What did you say?"

"I said Rainmaker, you deaf? That's what they told me they heard one of them call the man."

"Where is this man, where did he go?" the major inquired, but it sounded like an order.

"Go to hell, you Yankee bastard. I don't answer to you."

"Charley," the bartender pleaded. "You ought not to talk to the major that way. He just wants—"

The officer raised his hand again, then motioned for one of his men to stand next to the drunk.

"I know how to talk to Yankees. They're no better than rats in the streets. You see this?" Charley pointed at his vacant pantleg. "I lost that at Shiloh. There weren't no Yankees worried about me or my kind then, and I ain't seen nothing since to make me believe otherwise. So to hell with them."

"Ser-geant," the major shouted. The large soldier grabbed Charley and lifted him out of the chair. The old drunk's attempts to fight were squelched by the seizure of his arms.

"Now that I have your attention, let me tell you whom you're addressing. I am Major Miles Arthur Perry, Seventh Cavalry, Army of the United States of America. Currently on special dispatch from Fort Abraham Lincoln. Now, the name that you mentioned, associated with the death of those men out there, belongs to a man who is currently wanted as a traitor. The man's name is Clay Cole, otherwise known as the Rainmaker. He is the betrayer of the men led by Lieutenant Colonel George Armstrong Custer at the Little Bighorn river. Now, since you have said he was here a short time ago, it is now my duty as an officer to pursue this man and bring him back for court-martial. That is exactly what I am going to do."

Charley's eyes bulged in sober fear as the sergeant pulled a revolver and cocked the hammer.

"So, my confederate friend, if you don't tell me where the Rainmaker is, I will consider you in conspiracy with a fugitive and also a traitor to the United States, and I will have you shot right here in this saloon. Now, you tell me where he went."

The drunk could only shake his head, careful not to make any move that would provoke the major. "I don't know."

The officer nodded, and the sergeant tightened his grip on Charley's arm, ready to pull him toward the center of the room.

"I swear, I swear I don't know. All I heard was that he had rode off on a gray Palousey pony with a woman he took from those three out there. Some said that he figured to get a ransom for her from a mine owner. They rode off for the hills, toward Danger Ridge."

"Where?"

"That's what they call it around here," the bartender explained. "It's the north ridge, connecting the two ranges, that leads to the old mining hills. Some folks call it Danger Ridge."

The major slowly stepped toward the bartender. "How do I get to this Danger Ridge?"

Chapter Seven

The storm sounded like a snarling beast as it hovered above. A bolt of lightning shot down over the nearby hills. Thunder sliced through the clouds with the crackle of an old oak splitting apart, ending with a booming crash. The unrelenting storm saturated the mountainside. Claire clawed and dug her heels into the mire to gain footing up the slippery hills. Lightning allowed them to see into the dense foliage on their way to Jenks's cabin.

"Do you know where we are?" Claire shouted. She held out her arm, which Cole firmly grasped.

"Can't be much farther." He rammed the carbine stock into the mud as a support up the incline. "Just keep following me."

The downpour remained steady. Minutes turned into hours while they made their way through the forest.

A bright reflection from one of the flashes caught Claire's eye. "There's something over there." She pointed into the trees. Another flash revealed a shack with a small paned window.

"That should be it," Cole said as they neared the shack. When they got closer, he began to crouch, and then stopped behind a fallen tree. She crept to his side.

"What's the matter now?"

He motioned for her to lower her voice. "There's no light. Too early for even him to set in for the night." Cole slowly drew the revolver.

"You said you knew this man."

"That's been some time ago." He handed her the rifle and pointed for her to stay. He took long quick steps to the door. Looking through the glass, he saw no sign of anyone. He cocked the Colt and kicked in the door. Charging in, he fanned the gunsights at every corner. The storm's light showed it was vacant. Objects were strewn on the floor, but there was no sign of Jenks.

Rain swept into the shack. Cole motioned to Claire and she quickly ran into the shelter. He slammed the door, leaving only the window to allow lightning to illuminate the room.

"Where are you?" he called. Suddenly a cold

steel barrel poked into his mouth. He ripped the rifle free from its hold.

"Clay! Someone's here!"

He let out a long, exhausted sigh. "That was me, damn it. You nearly blew my damn head off."

"Well, I couldn't see. I'm sorry."

"Go sit down or something so I won't run into you, while I see if there's anything to make a fire with." Cole searched with his fingers, bumping into an overturned table, until he found himself at the back of the cabin. He bent down to find wet ashes in the fireplace. Another flash showed a hammock anchored between cornered walls. A blanket lay in the center. He picked it up and found a floppy brimmed hat under it. It looked like the one Jenks had worn the last time Cole had seen him.

Claire sat shaking in the middle of the cabin. Her quivering wasn't just from the cool dank air and her soaked clothes. She didn't understand why all these horrible things kept happening to her and she was afraid of what would happen next.

The dry warmth of a wool blanket wrapping around her interrupted her fearful thoughts. She sensed Cole standing over her. She heard another long sigh and was confident another lecture on what to do and why she should do it was sure to follow.

"No food or fires tonight. Are you all right?" he asked in a consoling tone.

She was surprised at his concern. "I'm not badly hurt, if that's what you mean. My ankle feels better with the walk. How is your hand?"

"Don't hurt much now."

"Where is your friend?"

"Wonderin' that myself. I found his hat back there. That's peculiar too, the last thing I would think him to do would be leave without it."

"Do you think something bad has happened to him?"

"Maybe. Place seems like it's been lived in lately, so whatever happened wasn't long ago." He unlaced the leggings and eased off his boots, grunting slightly with every motion. "He's probably lost in the storm. Jenks is getting on sixty now and folks thought him senile ten years back. But nothing I can do about it tonight. There's a hammock in back if you want to get comfortable. I never could get the hang of them things."

She stood and held out her hand to guide herself into the darkness. Stumbling into a wall, the coarseness of heavy twine rubbed against her face. She moved along its edge until she recognized the outline of the rope bed. A loud thud of something hitting the floor turned her head. The room lit up. Cole stood hatless, openshirted, gun in hand. Darkness returned. His low voice ordered, "First, take off your clothes."

She didn't move. She was powerless to stop him.

"You'll dry faster without them. With no fire,

it gets awful cold up here at night." She heard the sound of metal buttons being pulled loose from cloth, then the crumple of cotton collapsing. An aching grunt came from the floor. Wood creaked. A moment passed, then another. He wasn't moving toward her.

"Are you na—naked?" she asked cautiously.

"Yup."

"And what—what do you intend—I mean, what are your intentions? What are you going to do?"

"Rest."

"Are you going to sleep?"

"Nothing much else to do."

Guilt rang in her head, but she still wasn't going to remove her clothes, not for the second time in a day. Pneumonia was far preferable to losing her dignity.

A cool breeze through the cracks in the wall brought a chill to her soaked skin. She used the blanket as a towel, wiping it across the wet shirt, but every movement recoated her body. Her toes felt frozen. Her hair dripped water in her face. Combing it behind her head with her fingers wrung the drops down her back. Her cough was the last sign needed to convince her he was right again.

She closed her eyes and undid the buttons of the shirt, then peeled it from her shoulders. She pulled loose the knot which held the pants around her thin waist and released it, and they fell around her ankles. Stepping out of the pants, she quickly reached for the blanket to wrap around her nude figure. She couldn't locate it, so she opened her eyes and searched with her fingers. The texture of wool was in her grip. Before she could pull it up to her, lightning flashed outside, the light reflecting off her white flesh. She brought the blanket to her chin, but the cold air on her exposed backside made her aware she wasn't completely covered. She grasped the drooping excess with her free hand and now, completely enveloped, both hands full, she eased into the hammock.

The wool absorbed the moisture. Finally she was drying out. The shivers stopped. She was almost at ease. Cole had been right again.

The low grumble of thunder reminded her of the storm. She'd hated the sound since childhood. Cole sleeping on the floor wouldn't give her peace of mind either. She couldn't decide what was worse, this naked man so close to her or the thought of him on the damp wood without cover while she was warm. The thought wouldn't leave her alone. Another idea wouldn't go away either.

It was unthinkable, insane, forbidden by every rule she had been taught throughout her entire life as a lady in the East. But she wasn't under those ideal circumstances now and the only person she knew here was suffering because of her. If he were to fall ill from the exposure, how would he get her to the mine to join her beloved John?

The entire shack's interior was illuminated brighter than it had been all night. Cole's bare body lying curled on the wooden planks was the only thing she focused on. The brilliant light dimmed. Two breaths later, a crash shook the sheltering walls. Claire's feet found the floor. The picture of him shaking stained her eyes like a photograph. She used it as a map to crawl to him.

"Clay?"

"I'm not sleeping outside tonight. I promise, I can't see anything."

She took a long breath. "You are a gentleman, aren't you?"

There was a pause before his response. "If it means me getting a piece of that blanket, I can be anything you want me to be."

She settled on the floor as far away from him as she could stretch the end of the blanket. She couldn't believe where she was. What would her mother say right now? On the other hand, if a scolding were the only price to pay so she could be with her mother and leave this place, she'd gladly hear it.

"Thank you," he said. She was surprised by his gratitude. Maybe he was a gentleman.

More flashes beamed through the window. She pulled at the wool but found no slack. She inched closer to him. An edged splinter under her backside made her move even closer.

"I'd lay the table in the middle, but I doubt

either one of us would fit between the legs," he said.

"No. I don't think that's necessary. You told me you were a gentleman." A horrible thought popped into her head. "You wouldn't tell anyone, especially John, that I did this, would you?"

"Guess not. Why?"

"Swear to it, or I'll take the blanket right now."

"I said so, didn't I?" His voice sounded as if she held a gun. "You have my word on it."

Satisfied with the answer, she tried to sleep, but the frightening memories of the day wouldn't allow her. She rolled over on her side, which is how she normally slept, but even that didn't bring her any comfort. Although she lay naked next to this man, she felt very much alone. "Clay?"

"All right. I'll sleep outside."

"No, I don't want you to. I feel safer with you in here. Anyway, that's not what I was going to ask. Do you—do you think that those men that were shooting at us were—were shooting at you or me?"

He lifted his head. "Well, didn't want to say it, but I was thinking that too. I can think of why someone would want you alive, but I can't think of why they would want you dead. But that shot was aimed at you."

The pain in her stomach from the night before choked her breath again. "All I've wanted to do since I came west was to be with my husband, where I thought a wife should be. But every sign tells me that I shouldn't have come. John is absent at my arrival, three men I don't know say they will take me to him, you say they were lying and shoot them, my beautiful dress from New York is made a home for some rodent, and now it seems that someone is trying to kill me, I fall down a mountain, I'm nearly eaten by a monster. Why?" she mumbled through her tears.

"Can't say." He peered over his shoulder, leaning closer to her. She could sense the closeness of his body. "But I can say this. Things haven't been like I thought they'd be on this trip. But until I get you to that mine, I'm not going to let you out of my sight. I'm not going to have anything bad happen to you. Trust me. That's why I'm here."

His words soothed her mind. The tears stopped flowing. He gave her so much sanctuary from fear that she felt compelled to reach out to be held. Her probing hand rested along the firm muscles of his chest. He didn't resist the advance. His bandaged palm found her shoulder. The heat of his breath against her face guided her to the bristles on his cheek. His callused fingers ran down her side and touched her breast as if it was a delicate bloom. The warmth of his touch aroused her. She wondered if his kiss was as warm, and her primal desires pushed her to find out.

Tim McGuire

A flash showed her revealed breasts and the following blast sounded like a command from the Almighty, shocking her back to her senses. John's angry face screaming, "Adulteress!"; her father's scowl; her mother crying in disgrace filled her mind.

She fell back under the blanket. "Oh God, forgive me, please forgive me. I didn't come here for this," she wept.

The rain pounded the roof. The cold wind blew under the door. No further hardship could reprieve her soul from the sin of lust.

The blanket sagged around her. True to his word, he had left her side.

Chapter Eight

Blasts of gunfire tore Claire from her sleep. The splintered door flew open. Two men rushed out of the dawn's light into the cabin. Cole reached for his distant holster, but stopped at the ratchet of the repeater aimed at him.

"Easy there, Long-tall," said one of the men, letting out a hooting laugh. His front teeth were missing, allowing his tongue to slide through his lips like that of a snake. The thin beard and stringy long hair added to his repulsive manner. "Looks like we got two birds nesting here, Frankie."

Claire pulled the blanket from her bare shoulders up to her neck.

81

"My oh my. Have you have ever seen a prettier woman in your life?"

"Let's just get the gold, Bill."

"Gold?" questioned Cole.

"Don't you play us for fools, Long-tall. Your partner told us about the gold you have here."

"Partner?"

Bill raised the repeater to his shoulder.

"Oh, that partner. All right, I'll show you the gold, after the woman goes free."

Frankie pulled back the hammer of his long-barreled rifle. "You better show us that gold now, mister. While both of you are still alive."

"That's right, Long-tall. We may want a dip in that honey ourselves."

"Well, now that I know how it's going to be. Can I put my pants on?"

"Go ahead, as long as you don't have nothin' in them but your pecker."

Claire shielded her eyes from the naked Cole.

He stood to slip on his pants, then moved between both men. "You know, you're going to need something to haul it out of here with. There's over a ton buried under this shack."

Frankie and Bill's attention dropped to the floor; their gunbarrels wandered.

Cole backhanded Frankie in the face, knocking him backwards. Bill threw a punch, but Cole blocked the blow, looped his arm under Bill's elbow, and pulled up, stretching the joint backwards. Bill's agony was silenced when the heel of Cole's hand drove into his nose. Bill fell down, blood splashing his face.

Cole ducked away from Frankie's swinging rifle butt. In one movement, he stomped on the man's knee, sounding a loud crack. But the man still stood. Swinging his leg around just like the rifle butt, Cole struck his heel on Frankie's jaw, dropping him to the floor.

He looked back at Claire. "Get out of here."

She wrapped the blanket around her and ran to the door. Frankie started to raise his rifle. Cole quickly grabbed the barrel and snatched the knife from Frankie's belt, stabbing it into the man's chest. A loud gurgling wheezed from the body.

A reviving Bill caught Claire's attention.

He stood and started to aim his rifle.

"Clay! Behind you!"

Cole drew the knife and hurled it at his target. All but the handle plunged into Bill's throat. The rifle fired. The bullet hit a plank near Cole's head, spearing splinters into his left eyebrow. He fell to the floor, grabbing his head, rolling in pain.

Claire rushed to his side to help, but Cole's arm-wrapped head wouldn't allow her. She glanced at the wall and saw that Bill wasn't dead.

With blood spurting from his neck and face, Bill crawled toward her. Inching his way on elbows and knees, the dying man came nearer. Claire froze, not knowing what to do; Cole couldn't see the man crawling toward them. Bill reached out wildly at her and she recoiled in horror. He reached again, his bloody fingers latching onto the blanket.

He pulled it.

She fell back on the blanket, bringing him even closer to her and Cole. The other hand came from under his body, fingers stretching out for the holstered Colt.

She rose to her feet, her motion pulling Bill closer to the gun. His hand batted the butt, trying to pull it around. His eyes looked into hers, a cold stare from a dying man looking to take her and Cole with him.

She dropped the blanket, and on hands and knees raced to the pistol. Before she could reach it, Bill's hand wrapped around the butt, pulling it from the holster, and his finger nicked at the trigger. She pulled on the barrel, while its aim was at her heart. She pulled harder, but Bill's grip was frozen on the butt. His thumb climbed to the hammer. His thumbnail caught the edge, cocking it. His forefinger clipped the trigger.

Out of the corner of her eye she saw a blur of green moving toward her. The hammer released, flying toward the chamber, then stopped, jammed by Cole's finger.

Ripping the pistol from both their grasps, Cole looked at her, blood running from his left eyebrow down his face. He took a deep breath to say, "Get out."

Claire rose to her feet and ran toward the

door, grabbing the blanket, pulling it up in front of her naked body. She turned once at the door to see Cole looking at her, and Bill pulling the knife from his neck.

"Clay!" she yelled.

He turned and caught the blade in his bandaged palm, cutting the cloth as his fingers took hold of the edge. Cole clubbed Bill's head with the gun butt. He turned at her and yelled, "Go."

Claire ran out the door and saw movement in the nearby brush. She raced back into the cabin.

Cole swung the gun butt into Bill's head over and over. Blood flew in the air with each stroke. She watched him, muted by the sight. With each impact of the butt, Bill's body showed less life. Cole slammed it into the bloodied skull until it lodged deep. He grabbed the man's neck for leverage to pull the gun free. He looked back at her standing at the door. He was shaking, his arm quivered.

She stood, unable to move from the spot. She'd not seen him like this, like a wild animal. His appearance beamed anger, perhaps intended at her.

She announced, "There's another one. Out in the bushes!"

He jumped up, pistol in hand, and ran at her.

She froze and closed her eyes. He pulled her away, the force throwing her onto something on the floor.

"How many?" he yelled.

She didn't think to answer, thankful to be alive. The lump under her was Frankie's corpse.

She rolled off him to see Cole run to the small paned window. He peered out and poked the Colt through the glass to aim. He pulled back the Colt's hammer and pointed it out the window. He paused and uncocked the pistol.

"I've seen that head before." A smile creased his face. "Jenks?"

Claire climbed to her feet and ran to the window next to Cole.

The man emerged from the brush. "Cole? That you?"

"He's a colored man?" Claire asked, surprised.

"Yeah, I guess he is," Cole answered. "But don't tell him that. You've never seen hornets get that stirred up." Cole tucked the pistol in his pants and went out the door. He walked into the bushes toward the man outside.

"I thought I'd seen that saddle before," Jenks said, smiling as he and Cole approached each other. The black man had gray hair lining each side of his bald scalp. Suspender straps over his checkered shirt held up dirt-colored pants over a protruding stomach. His stocky frame limped slightly toward the cabin. "Did you kill them both?"

Cole nodded.

A frown crossed Jenks's face as he talked. "You smashed my window. Had to send all the way to St. Louie for that, took four months. You didn't tear nothin' else up, did you? Took me most of last summer and all this spring to keep that shack standing. I don't want to have to be doing double work on it."

"It's good to see you too, Jenks," Cole answered. "Oh, don't thank me for saving your life. And what's this story about gold, and being your partner?"

"Save my life? Hell, I told that gold story to save my own neck. Knew those boys would come back for it. I was ready to get the jump on them when they came out. Then your friend came out instead. Who the hell is that, anyway?"

"Hel-lo," Claire called from inside the cabin.

The frown deepened on Jenks's face. "Good God Almighty. Is that what I think I heard?"

Claire shed the blanket and climbed into her pants, threw on her shirt, which, untucked, resembled a nightgown. She walked out of the cabin and greeted both men with as gracious a smile as she could muster.

"Mrs. Claire Rhodes, meet Lucious Jenkins."

Claire offered her hand, but Jenks slowly shook his head. "Ain't nothin' a man ever gave a woman that she ever give back the same." Jenks looked at Cole. "What you doing bringing one of those up here? You know what they do to a man. Can't you just take care of your nature in a bed somewheres else? You had to bring her to my place?"

"Jenks—"

"And a Mrs. too. There's going to be some mister aiming at you and he's going to hit me."

"Jenks, shut up before I knock you down," Cole ordered, and the old man huffed his lips together. "I'm taking Mrs. Rhodes to her husband's silver mine. I thought I would come here 'cause I figured you'd know where it is. But if you want me leaving, I'll take their horses and we'll go now."

Jenks stared at Cole, then at Claire, then at the ground. "Guess I wouldn't mind the talking," he admitted.

Cole and Claire greeted the old man's decision with a grin, then Claire's eyes caught a familiar sight.

"Oh my, it's Pepper."

Both men looked confused "What?" they asked in unison.

"Your horse," she answered, pointing at the Appaloosa tied to the nearby branches, next to two roans. "I named him that because his rump appears sprinkled with it."

"You named my horse? Without me knowing it?"

"What does it matter if I alone call him that? You don't have to if you don't wish to."

Jenks shook his head at Cole. "Hell, Cole. Now she's naming your horse. I told you 'bout those—what they do." He paused a moment, then looked at the oversize shirt on Claire and the shirtless Cole. "Anything else of your'n that she give a name to?"

Cole raised his fist, to which Jenks only shook his head.

"Come on, let's get these two out of my house. We'll feed the varmints with them."

"You're not going to give them a Christian burial?" Claire asked.

"I told you before, these type of men are not churchgoers."

"No, but we are," she retorted, then paused. "Well, at least I trust we are all Christians. And as Christians, it is our duty to see that even 'these type of men' receive a decent burial. And if you won't do it, then I will."

Both men stood stunned at her speech, but neither of them answered.

"Mr. Jenkins, where is your shovel?"

Jenks looked at Cole with an even more disapproving grimace. "You had to bring one of those up here."

"Shut up and get your shovel before she gets her second wind."

Claire now aimed her shocked face at Cole.

"I'm gonna do it!" he answered before she could say a word.

"My, you must have one powerful punch of womanhood to be ordering men around like mules."

"Shut up, Jenks."

"Yes ma'am, you sure must have the smell about you. Anything else you'd like that Mr. Cole could get for you? Wouldn't want him to get in your bad mind no more."

"Are we going to bury these men or yammer all day?" Cole said as he walked toward the cabin.

Claire thought for a moment. "A bath and a hot meal would do wonders for my disposition, Mr. Jenkins."

"Yes'm, I could see it would." Jenks pointed down a long slope behind the shack. "Down the side there's a crick runs into a pond. Snakes there won't bother no human folk. A barrel of salted pig grease is by the side—gets the ticks off of you." He walked toward the cabin. "By the time you're done, I'll have the rest of the makings of son-of-a-bitch stew."

Major Miles Perry led his squad toward the narrow ledge entering Danger Ridge. He glanced at the sun directly overhead; they had ridden all night and morning, but for patriots in pursuit of a traitor, the hardships of fatigue and hunger were secondary to duty.

Buzzards in circular flight caught his eye. They were gliding over the ridge; a sure marking they were on the right path.

As the column entered the ledge below the ridge, blood lined a path to the other end of the ridge. Perry spotted objects up on the high rocks. The figures resembled men lying motionless. He raised his hand and the order was given to dismount.

"Fan out. There must be more here." He climbed the rocks toward the bodies. The large birds flew from the rocks with the approach.

Perry came on the first body, a young man. Bullet holes in the forehead and chest had been enlarged by the scavengers. Red tissue blotted the torn face. The skin was pale and bloated. The right eye had been pecked out, the left remained open in a frozen stare. Perry knelt, removing his glove to touch the boy's cheek. It had a leathery wrinkle where it was pulled.

Lieutenant Andrew Moore came up next to him, turning his head at the repulsive sight. "Good place for an ambush," Moore said, looking at the tall peaks. "Hard to know when this happened."

"I've seen a lot of bodies, Lieutenant. More than days you've been alive," Perry said as he rose. "This one's been dead less than one of those days."

"Major," came a shout from a soldier on the ledge. The two officers descended to where he was standing. "Spent casings. Eight of them, sir."

"The caliber?" the major confidently inquired.

"They're .44/.40s, sir. Winchester make."

A brief grin crinkled the major's face. "Very good then. We're close to our objective. Prepare to mount."

"Wait," the lieutenant blurted.

Perry turned abruptly. His creased brow and cliched jaw were meant to remind the junior officer of his rank.

"Begging the major's pardon, sir, but I think we must reconsider going any further away from our destination. We're twenty days out of Fort Lincoln. Our orders are to meet the payroll train fifty miles from here in less than two days."

"I'm well aware of our orders, Lieutenant Moore." Perry turned back to the column and stepped into the stirrup. "Mount."

"With all due respect, sir, I feel this pursuit could endanger our mission." Moore walked close to Perry and whispered, "I know what this man Cole means to you. We've all heard the accounts of Colonel Custer's battle and your part in it. But it's over, and I'm afraid your obsession with Cole's capture could take us miles into unmapped territory."

"Are you saying we should fear the unknown? The United States Army? I won't listen to this," Perry remarked with contempt. "Column—"

"You don't even know where this man is, what he looks like now. You said yourself that you hadn't seen him since that day. A coward will change his ways many times to avoid being caught."

Perry's arm pulled back the reins and bent forward directly in the young lieutenant's face. "A traitor, yes, but Cole is no coward. No braver man fought renegades than he. I know what he's like. I know how he moves, how he walks, talks, and eats. Most of all, I know how he thinks. For three years I have hunted this man.

For three years I have lived with the memory of that day. You were just a schoolboy then, still in the academy. All you could think of was how your uniform looked on parade to the females you hoped to entertain at parties, and later escort to your bed, while real soldiers were fighting the savage day and night, showing what it really meant to be a man. Men fighting shoulder to shoulder, depending on each other for their strength, trusting each other with their lives. Victory after victory we won, until this man broke that trust. And men lay slaughtered by the savage. Now, fate has given me the chance I've needed to see justice done. I intend to use it in every way I can."

"But sir—"

"There'll be no further discussion, Lieutenant Moore. The order has been given to mount."

Moore stepped away, his head bowed in disappointment.

"We're moving on. I suggest you follow my orders, Lieutenant. If I find you out of sight of the column, I will consider you a deserter and have you court-martialed."

Moore's head shot up. He slowly saluted his superior. "Yes sir," he said through gritted teeth.

Perry raised his arm high and pointed forward.

Chapter Nine

Towering pines shaded the small pond from the late afternoon sun. Claire, having scrubbed away the grit from the last two days, enjoyed the relaxing peace of her surroundings. She tried to clear her mind of the horrible scenes she'd witnessed.

Although it was common knowledge that this part of the country had yet to be civilized, she hadn't expected such a crude and primitive life. Men killing men just to exist wasn't what she had expected. Perhaps Cole and the others were right; this was no place for a lady from the East. That's what her father told her as well. His view of her was the same as when she was still a young girl. But she was a grown woman now, and a wife; that might be the hardest memory for her to keep in mind.

She concentrated on the refreshing cool water soothing her scorched skin. She closed her eyes as she floated, listening to the serenade of the birds, the trickling of the stream into the pond, the breeze whistling through the leaves.

"Claire!"

The familiar tone of Cole's shout was no comfort. She quickly submerged herself, raising only her head above the surface. Though shielded by the water, she wrapped her arms to cover her body. "What do you want? I haven't any clothes on."

"That's why I'm here—I mean, I've got some clothes for you. Some woman clothes."

"And how did you come by them?" She peeked through the bushes to try to see him, but the brush was too thick.

"When we were burying them two, Jenks remembered a trunk that he'd buried. It was from settlers some years back. They were wiped out by the Cheyenne. Guess that bunch didn't have much need for white man clothes."

"You expect me to wear someone else's clothes? Something that your friend stole from a dead woman?"

"Figured it was better than what you were wearing. Anyway, it ain't stealing. He was just salvaging it. He does that a lot. Hell, there's no telling what else he's got buried up here. There probably is a ton of gold he's packratted away somewhere. Anyhow, you wear what you want. I just thought—never mind. I'll leave them here on the bushes for when you get out."

She sensed a caring in his voice that she had heard once before.

"Supper will be in about an hour."

"I hope the taste isn't as foul as the name."

"Really, it's not too bad. Jenks is a pretty good cook."

"What's in it?"

"You don't want to know. It will be dark come an hour. Don't dawdle."

"Clay," she called. "I feel there is something that must be said, and now seems the best time, since we're alone. We are alone, aren't we?"

"Go on."

"With all that has happened to me, as scared as I was, I needed someone last night. Someone to hold me close, to protect me. I wanted to feel a man's touch, and then I was overwhelmed by the moment. Fate put us together. I thank the heavens that I can say I remained faithful to my vows. But I can't escape the guilt I feel now. I am married to John and I must try to redeem my faithfulness to him. As a wife, I must do that. I don't blame you. And I want to apologize for my—my—indiscretion. I still would like to be a friend to you. I'm hopeful you can under-stand that." An anxious silence followed. "Clay?"

"I heard you. You're right, it had to be said. Guess you had more guts than me to say it first."

There was a long pause before he spoke again. "One hour, Mrs. Rhodes."

She took the formality as a signal that there would be a change between them; one she didn't know that she truly wanted. She rinsed the tears from her face.

After his footsteps had faded, she slowly rose out of the pond. Quickly, she darted into the high brush.

Clothes dangled from the branches of a fallen tree. The plain gray skirt and blouse were hardly the style shown in *Godey's Lady's Book*. She took the camisole, gazed at its size, and slipped it on. The fit on top was tailored for a more blessed woman. There was no corset. She stepped into the skirt, which wrapped nicely around her waist, and in another moment she flung her curled locks over the blouse's collar and buttoned up the front. She pulled her brooch from the pants pocket and pinned it inside the blouse.

The dimming light guided her up the hill. As she sighted the cabin, she took notice of fresh dirt a short distance away. Realizing what she was looking at, she forced her eyes away, not wanting any further reminder of the terrible things she'd seen that day.

"What the hell do I have to do?"

Carl Hensley ran his fingers through his thinning red hair while watching his boss hobble on a cane in front of him.

"What do I have to do? You told me that you could take this man, and you come back telling me that you've lost three more men to the gun of this Rainmaker."

"I told you, I think I got the woman. Ain't that what you said you wanted?"

"You think so!"

"I couldn't tell for sure. She fell down the slope, and it was hard to make out if she was moving between the trees. Kept firing as long as I could, till—well, till Cole came up the ridge like I said. I did the best I could."

The vested man took a long puff on his cigar and eased into a chair. "You're an ass, Carl. Cole has proven that."

The redhead's jaw clenched.

"When I hired you, you guaranteed me you could get what I wanted with just you and your brother. I gave you Jeb and his boys, all to get one woman. All she has is some saddle tramp. Now six men are dead, you come here with your tail between your legs, and Claire Rhodes is still out there, maybe dead, maybe not, carrying a fortune. And you tell me you did the best you could! Goddamn, how much worse would it have been if you had done badly?"

Hensley inhaled a long breath through his flared nostrils. It had been a long time since he'd been talked to like a child, but he knew he had it coming. "I'll get her and that son of a bitch Cole come sunup."

The boss laughed. "Hell, what for? That's the

one thing you were right about. Something tells me she's still alive, and if they rode through Danger Ridge, it's a pretty sure bet that Cole is bringing her to the mine. It seems I didn't need you at all."

Hensley put on his Stetson and pulled it tight. "I guess I'll draw my pay and head out then."

"Stay here. Besides, the pay you have coming won't pay for the shells you spent. I may still have use for you. This affair is just a side track to the work I really want done. There's still a lot of land I don't own yet, and I need your talent to help me get it." A smirk creased his lips. "When Bill and Frank come back after running off that old nigger, you can take them along with Pete, Tom, and Ben and clean out the rest of these hills of miners."

"What about your partner? He takes a dim view of killing."

"To hell with him. I'll handle it. You just do as you're told. If all goes as planned, before long I'll be the richest man in these hills."

As darkness fell on the mountain, Claire pushed the cabin door open. She found Jenks hovering over a pot in the glowing fireplace. The flames lit up the small room. It was the first time she took notice of its interior of wood-plank walls masoned with mud. She saw the hammock anchored on the wall, along with a variety of ropes, pickaxes, shovels, pans, and cups. Cole sat at a table of chiseled timber. The glow of the fire lit up his eyes as it had in the cave. His expression distanced her. She took a deep breath and stepped into the cabin.

"Fits you mighty good," Jenks said with a satisfied grin. "Thought it would when I first saw you."

Claire examined the shape of the plain gray blouse and skirt on her. "The hem is too long. But I must say, it feels better to dress as a lady again. Thank you, Mr. Jenkins, for your kindness in thinking of me."

"Couldn't use it nohow. Find your place, stew's boiling ready."

She sat down at the table across from Cole. He stared into the fire, dodging her eyes. She looked at the pot and then at Jenks. "Smells delicious. I'm told you are quite a good cook."

"Cooked for forty men in my trail days. Never heard none of them complain about it. Damn good for that bunch." Jenks hooked the ladle to the pot. Kneeling on the floor, he pulled up a loose plank to remove a large jug from the hole. "Hey Cole. This is the best squeeze I've done since I can recall." He placed the jug in front of Cole and returned to the pot.

"You still makin' shine? Up here?"

"Took me a spell to find what I needed. Tell me if it don't taste like the hooch that gets sold east. The six-bit stuff they put in a bottle, with fancy writing stuck to it."

"What's it from?"

Jenks grinned. "Taste it first."

Cole pulled out the cork, hooked the jug with his finger, and slung it over his shoulder. He raised it to his lips and gulped in a mouthful. He stopped, held his breath; his face puffed first white, then red. His nostrils flared, his eyes watered, and his neck bulged as he swallowed.

Claire watched intently, thinking his reaction to the liquor resembled the pained anguish of the men she'd seen killed that day.

His gritted teeth showed through his parting lips and he loudly belched and coughed, trying to gain his breath. "Oh! That's good."

"Leaves you a good burn, don't it?"

"That it does. Best I've had in a while." Cole took two smaller swigs, belched again, and returned the jug to the table.

"Really?" Claire asked, sniffing at the spout.

"That's a fact," Jenks proclaimed proudly. "You don't want any of that. That's not any sassparilly. That's a man's drink."

"Is that a fact?" she lashed back. "May I have some?"

"No," Cole ordered. "We just cleaned the place up from the mess of them two this morning."

"I'm sure that not only men can enjoy a satisfying drink."

The two men looked at each other, then Jenks nodded his approval.

Claire raised the jug with two hands, first to sniff the spout once more. Then she closed her eyes, took a delicate sip, paused, then took another, then another. The abrasive liquid shot through her mouth like fire, but as the harsh taste singed her tongue, it left a lingering flavor of berries. Squinting her eyes from the tartness, she smacked her lips and took a longer drink from the jug. She wiped her tongue against her palate, drew a deep breath, and exhaled through puckered lips. "This tastes like wine. Very fruity wine."

Cole and Jenks leaned closer to her.

"Although it doesn't seem properly fermented yet. But it does have a good taste to it."

Both men looked in amazement at her, then at each other.

"How you feel, dizzy some?" Jenks asked.

Claire shook her head "No. We have this with dinner all the time at home. But you're right, it's not for children." She smirked at Cole.

Jenks laughed. "A woman that can drink squeeze, never thought to see it."

"Stew ready yet?" Cole grunted.

Jenks pulled three plates off the wall, blew out the dust, and ladled out the stew. He placed the full plates in front of the two at the table. The hearty smell of meat steamed through Claire's nose. Cole immediately shoveled a spoon into the stew and swallowed a mouthful.

She stared at him. "I don't suppose grace is observed here, but today is the Sabbath."

Cole shook his head and ate another mouthful. "Food gets cold too quick." She bowed her head, giving a moment of thanks for her blessings, and ended by crossing herself.

"You a religious woman?" Jenks asked as he sat at the table and began eating.

She nodded. "Aren't you a believer in religion, Mr. Jenkins?"

"Oh, I think religion's a fine thing. Trouble starts when folks take it serious."

Claire's throat tightened. She couldn't decide if it was from his remark or the taste of the stew. She chewed the soft meat and swallowed.

"How do you mean that?"

"All their talk about God, 'bout God being like some man, giving and taking away things from people. Men waving a book around saying they know what God's thinking and that if they pay them—and pray to God—that God will be on their side of things. Don't know how people can think that, something giving life to everything so their own kind can take what they want as long as they thank God for it. Weak, weak is all they is." He gulped a mouthful of stew and kept talking, bits of food slipping out of his mouth. "People, long time back, lookin' at all that was around them, couldn't figure out why things got to be the way they was. Couldn't think that it just happened, so when younguns started to ask 'em how things got to be that-a-way, they thought up God."

Claire noticed Cole silently shaking his head. "So, you don't believe there is a God, a heavenly father?"

Cole rolled his eyes. "Now you done it."

"Oh, I believe in God. But he's no man thing. Men think that God invented the world. Hell, God *is* the world. You live by yourself, where you can just watch things, and you see God. The rocks and dirt were here long before folks walked on them. Trees that took ten man-lives to grow didn't raise up so men could cut them down. Water ain't there for you to drink it. First ones did—probably killed them. But they kept up drinkin' it till it didn't kill them no more. That's what God is—everything changing— learning to live with what you got and what you can get. God don't give nothin' with your hand out. You got to go and get it. Got to work hard— everytime you can—and you best be turning and looking because something else out there's doing the same. If you're not doing what you can to get your share, then something's going to sneak up on you—steal your food—take over your home—eat your children. That's the way God wants it."

The gas building inside her started to exit her nose and forced her mouth open, which she quickly covered. "I apologize for asking. I was always taught never to discuss a person's politics or religion. Why I asked, I don't know."

"Don't mind telling you what I think. Don't hurt me none."

"Yes, well . . . I'd rather talk about where John's mine is and how we get there."

"Don't know. Never heard of no John Rhodes up here."

"What?" she asked, staring at Cole.

He looked at Jenks, who shrugged his shoulders.

"I can't have come all this way to be lost," she exclaimed.

Cole looked surprised as well. "You mean you don't know where it is? Figured you'd know all that was around here."

"Know most of what's around here. Never heard that name talked. Most fact is, here the boom is over. Lot of men up digging holes everywhere, panning every stream once-a-times, finding gold and then silver, but now the hills are played out. Everyone went east back over the mountains to Leadville."

"I can hardly believe it."

"Think I'm lying? Here," Jenks said, getting up and reaching back down into the hole in the floor. He pulled out a newspaper wrapped as a bundle. Unfolding the paper, he pulled out a piece of what looked to be meat, sniffed it, wrinkled his nose as if it were spoiled, and casually tossed it into the fire. "I remember the man saying this said so when he give it to me."

He gave the newspaper to Cole, who seemed dumbfounded at the printing. He handed the newspaper over the table to Claire.

"What's it say?"

"Can't you read?" she said, still upset, until she noticed Cole's eyes dart downward, and realized the accuracy of her remark. Feeling a fool again, she paused, unfurrowed her brow, and

Independence Public Library

said, "I'm sorry. I didn't mean it as it sounded."

The reeking newspaper turned her attention back to the point of the matter. After a few moments she looked again at both men.

"Well, is it true?" Jenks asked.

"All it reports is about a man named Tabor and the fortune he's made from some mines. One, it says," she glanced back at the newspaper, " 'is rich in silver ore like no other.' "

"Told you."

"But it doesn't prove that John is there."

"Most all the mines here shut down 'cept those owned by the big comp'ny. Man named Larsen holds those."

Claire recognized the name. "Hoyt Larsen?"

"Larsen's all I know. 'Mister' Larsen they call him."

"That would be John's partner. That must be where John's mine is."

"If that be your man, I don't want no part of you. It was him that sent those two dogs after me—Larsen."

"What are talkin' about, Jenks?" asked Cole.

"The two you killed here. They came around sayin' Larsen owned the land now. Told them they been told a lie. I owned this stake and was staying. Then they said Larsen would pay me to leave if I just come with him. Knew that was a lie too."

"Perhaps not. I have to say that I don't know Hoyt Larsen that well, but I do know my husband, and he's an honorable businessman. He would have paid you and found you another place for your home."

"Ain't no white men gonna find a darkie a place to stays but the grave. Specially those that talk back. I lived that truth all my life. No, I like it fine right here."

"He's right, those two aren't the kind you send on a business call," Cole said to her, then turned to Jenks. "So what did they do, bushwhack you?"

"Hell yes, while I was handlin' my nature in the trees. Grabbed me—wouldn't let me finish. Thought I'd be dead in the night. Before they could take me where to do me in, they found the horse. Knew I'd seen the Double C on the saddle before. That's when I told them that was my partner's and there was gold in my shack where he was. Turned out to be your horse."

"And you talk about preachers thinkin' up stories," mused Cole.

"Well, I'm confident it's not John that would be doing this to you or anyone else. I can't speak as to why, but I'm sure it can all be explained." Her excitement at hearing something to do with her husband showed in her voice. "Tomorrow, when we arrive, we can settle the entire matter, and an apology will be given." She looked down at her plate. "I feel an appetite now more than ever. May I have more?"

Jenks refilled her plate.

She started scooping the stew into her mouth as she had seen the men do. She felt like an animal, but she enjoyed the stew's taste more with every spoonful, and couldn't stop herself. Both men finished their food and Jenks went to refill the plates. As soon as he did, she held her cleaned plate out to request more.

"You must have been hungry," an astonished Cole stated.

"I haven't eaten anything of any substance since my last night in Denver. This is very good once you get used to the taste of it. I don't know why it's earned the name you give it. What's the recipe?"

"I told you, you don't want to know."

"Excuse me, I wouldn't have asked if I didn't want to know."

"Wasn't it you just sayin' that you don't know why you ask questions you're sorry for askin'?"

"This isn't about those subjects. Most cooks are proud of their recipes. I thought it polite to ask."

"Go ahead, Jenks. I'm done with mine."

Jenks placed another helping in front of her and sat down. "Hands on the cow trails would call it lawyer stew, named for them that truly pick at your bones. But it got called what it is for the son of a bitch that told what's in it." Both of them waited for her reaction.

She continued gulping the stew down, confused as to why they stared at her. "And?"

"Well, we don't have no cows up here, so I used what I could get. Got a fresh carcass from some Utes for some tobacco. First, I cut the head off, easier to pull the eyes out that way. I cleaned them, then the tongue, and the brain. Then you strip the meat with the heart, lungs, liver, short gut, and don't forget the oysters, that's the taste, and most of what else you can throw in the pot. But not the stomach; that truly is nasty in one of them animals."

She stopped eating.

"Then, you dice it up small so's you can't tell what it is. Then throw in some onions, mushrooms, turnips if you can find them. Cook it all most the day and eat it once the sun goes down. Normally you do that so them that lose their dinner don't spoil it for the rest of them eatin'."

She sat there with an unswallowed mouthful, then slowly choked it down. "I thought the taste was different."

"What?" Cole said with surprise. "Knowing that doesn't bother you?"

She shook her head and took another bite. "When one lives on Chesapeake Bay, one learns to eat crab. When my family would have crab for dinner, the meat was nicely prepared and we would eat from a dessert dish. Afterwards, I used to sneak off into the kitchen, where our Negro servants showed me how to really eat them. We'd tear those crabs apart and eat everything but the shell. The best taste was the mustard. It was delicious. Once you learned what the mustard is in a crab, nothing bothers you."

Cole gave a look of disbelief at Jenks. "Don't

aim that at me. You brung her," the old man said.

Claire took delight in their dismay.

Cole went to the fire, took a tin cup from the wall, and poured coffee in it from the hanging pot.

Jenks chuckled and shook his head while looking at her. "Thought I'd seen most things in life up here. Just shows, nobody seen it all."

"Just how long have you lived up here, Mr. Jenkins?"

"Any woman of your kind that drinks hooch and gobbles down son-of-a-bitch stew can call me Jenks."

She smiled.

"Let's see. With all the times back and forth livin' else places, it's been close to twenty years, I'd say."

"It is beautiful. Is that why you like it here?"

"Wouldn't stays here if'n I didn't. It's pretty now. But in six weeks, the snow'll be at your knees. Have to work to keep livin'. Snow and wind kills lots of critters. But it can make life too. I remember more than ten years back, snow was so deep, folks up here couldn't open their doors. Men with their women had to stay insides so long, by the next summer they was havin' babies."

Claire thought of the previous night. She bowed her head, trying not to show herself blushing. When she looked up, Cole dipped his head to stare at his coffee.

"The sight of the hills is pretty. That, and being without no other folk here gives you time. Time you don't get most places. That's why I like it."

"So then, what are our plans for the trip tomorrow?" she asked.

"Are you still wanting to go? There may be more of this morning's two waiting for us on the way."

"Of course. Anyway, I'll remind you of what you said. That nothing would happen to me while you're around."

He took a deep breath and held it. His nostrils flared when he let it out.

"You should have seen him fighting those men. How bold he was to fight them alone, hitting them and kicking them. They weren't a match for him."

"I'd just as soon not do it over, if I can help it."

"Yeah, Cole, he is a good fighter. Was too when he was in the troopers. I seen him fight when he was in a scrape with some running their mouths at him. When he'd take on a man, he could fight better with his feet than they could with their fists." Jenks chuckled. "Hey Cole, You remember when you and me and Hickok went into Platte Falls?" Jenks turned to Claire. "You see, the bar man, he didn't like me coming in there. Old Wild Bill, he took that man by the shirt and said he didn't want to drink in his bar. Took two bottles off the shelf and a table and chairs off the floor, and we went and drank in the street. You remember?"

Cole nodded. "I remember."

Claire smiled at the grin on Jenks's face.

"That bar man, he didn't take kindly to being talked to that-a-way, and he sent some of his boys to take back his belongings. But Cole there, he made them boys wish they'd never come outside. He put all three on the dirt before they could take a swing. One he made cry. Didn't you?"

Cole frowned. "I was half drunk then, and I also remember being shot at."

"Yeah, that be true. Wild Bill nearly didn't leave that town. Got shot three times, but not a one put him down." Jenks paused. "Wild Bill, now he is a man too."

"Was one," said Cole. "A man put a slug through his head in Deadwood almost three years ago."

Jenks looked shocked. "No. Wild Bill dead?"

Cole nodded again. "Happened almost a month after Cust—" He stopped.

"Well, I guess I knew that day would have to come. Anyway, Cole's a good fighter. Learned it from some Chinaman, didn't you? What was his name, Doo? Boo? Something like that?"

"Ding. Never could say his other names."

"Yeah, that's it. This Chinaman was peaceful, but he could fight when them drunks would rile him. When I saw what he could do, I learned quick to call him mister. He learned you them moves, didn't he?"

"I picked up a few things, except his patience. That's what he tried to teach most."

"Ah, that's no good out here, anyway. Patience get you killed out here. Got to fight when you have to. Like you did."

Claire looked at the silent Cole as he stood by the fire. There was an uneasiness about him despite Jenks's praise. Her intuition told her it was from their conversation at the pond.

"Anyway," Jenks continued, "still can be a rough trip there."

"I'm not scared anymore. Not with my protector by me," she said.

Cole threw the rest of the coffee in the flames and started for the door. "Guess I need to tend to the horses for the trip." As he pulled the door open, he turned. "Getting late for an early start in the morning. I'll bed down outside." The door shut behind him.

She sensed his cold voice was a sign that whatever closeness she had gained from him during the trip was now lost.

"What's got him now?"

"I'm afraid it's my doing. There must be something that I've said, and I think I know what."

"Don't fret Cole. He's an inside man—keeps it inside him. He's always been that way, ever since I known of him."

"That I've learned. I've asked him questions, but he ignores them."

"Guess if you ain't paid to know them things, then it's not your business."

She smiled. "That's the same as he said. Do you know him well?"

"Ain't nobody knows Cole good. He was that way when he was with the troopers, and even after Custer."

"He spoke of that too. What happened to him? Was he at the battle?" she asked.

"Yeah, I heard he was there. Some folks say he run when the injuns came. But I never believed it."

"What did he tell you?"

"Never asked him. Don't know if I really want to know. Not with the army after him and all."

"Like a criminal or something?"

Jenks nodded as he lit a small pipe. "Treason, they call it."

Claire was shocked by the word.

"But I don't pay it much mind. He's a friend. Always will be. He might tell you some about himself."

"He doesn't talk about himself to me."

"It takes time. Cole is like the stories my mama told me about men in the old Africa land. When they get cut or something—hurt bad—they pick at it. Make it hurt worse—both outside and inside—till they can stand all the pain it gives. They get used to it—till it can't hurt no more."

"Until they're numb to it," she reflected.

"That's right. Cole's a lot like that. Them stories about him running at the battle—he's just standing the pain right now. Was that way when his daddy died off too."

"Oh. How did that happen?"

Jenks took a long drag on his pipe, then held the bowl in his hand. "Killed in the war. Cole was a boy with his daddy's troop down in Texas. Sent him there after his mama died. Taught him the army life, which was all his daddy knowed. He learned to beat the drum for the lines so's he could stay. The way Cole tells it, his daddy fell right in front of him from a reb's ball in the gut. Took him two days just to die. Bad thing was, the war had been over for near a month too."

"Oh, how awful," Claire said, imagining the scene.

Jenks nodded. "Something like that burns deep in a man's mind. Takes a long time to get it out of you." Pipe smoke bellowed from his nose. "Only place for him to go was the army. So they kept him, made a trooper out of him. Would have taken out the hate on normal folks, so the army pointed him at the injuns, so as to take it out on them."

"Such an experience. No wonder it would make one bitter." The comparison with John came to mind. "Did you ever know if he—if there was a woman he cared for?"

Jenks sheepishly grinned. "When we were

riding, there were a lot of them. Course, Cole liked doing his nature with whores, like all men do. But he stopped that once he took up with one. Found her in a Wyoming cattle town. She was a smart one, you could tell it, too. Once she saw him, she wanted him. He took to her like a crow does corn. She would order him around and he'd follow like a little puppy dog. That's what split us. She was gonna give up whorin' and theys was shakin' up together." He inhaled on the pipe. "The next time I saw him was a summer later. He was on his own again. Asked him about her. He gave me the look that Cole gives when he don't want to talk. Sometime later, when he was all drunked up, he told me about her, how he was going to be a papa and how one day, when he was gone, there be a fire. He never talked about her again."

Claire shut her eyes, remorseful of her first judgment of Cole. "What was she like?"

Jenks tapped out the pipe on his chair. "She looked a lot like you."

Claire's eyes opened wide as she slowly faced him.

"Cole wouldn't tell you. But you knowing this might make you see why he don't talk about himself. Might make you see why he's that-a-way."

She stared into the fire, then smiled at Jenks. She placed her hand on his, feeling the hard, wrinkled skin. Although she had been taught to be fair-minded, she also had been told colored people weren't meant to be in her station in life. Now she was ashamed for once thinking it. A confession would be awkward; she'd settle her conscience inside. "You are a very wise man."

He smiled back. "That's what living a long time gets you." He rose from his chair and took a step toward the hammock. "And living a long time makes you sleepy."

"Was there a lady in your past?"

Jenks stopped with the question. He looked at the floor, his lip twitched. "I've knowed a whole lot of 'em in my days on this earth."

"But none took your heart, I suppose." Her own smirk faded with the solemn change in his face.

"I had a squaw once, a Crow. Traded three ponies for her."

"You bought her?"

Jenks answered her amazement with a quick, stern glance. "Them was the best saddle ponies I had at the time. Was a might good price for a skinny woman in the winter." He grinned. "But she proved to be worth the price. No white woman, evens if they were colored, could do the chores she did. Hunt, cook, clean your clothes, wash your back, and keep you warm at night. Wasn't much else a man could be wantin'."

Claire enjoyed the delight on his face. "What became of her?"

"She got swelled with a baby, so I took her back to her own."

The notion of leaving a woman expecting a

child, whatever her race, appalled Claire. "You did what?"

Jenks rubbed his face and slowly sank on the hammock and closed his eyes. "I didn't know nothin' about having no young-uns."

"So you abandoned her?"

He peeked back at her. "The Crow knew how young-uns are born. She did it fine without me. Had us a son. A big one too."

Claire shook her head. "You talk of it so casually. I would think you would want to be near your son. To be a father to him."

He raised his head and stared her in the eye. "I ain't no father and I ain't no husband. She knowed that. I took her back to her own for that." He laid his head down. "They took to him just fine." He lowered his voice as if only talking to himself. "Anyway, the boy, Choate, he want nothing to do with me."

Although Claire couldn't condone such a thought, she realized that the personal matters of others under circumstances she had not known, weren't hers to judge.

"Sleep near the fire. Gets cold—"

"Cold up here at night? Yes, I've learned that much." Claire sat at the table, thinking about the stories Jenks had told about himself and Cole. Her thoughts turned to John. Tomorrow she would see him at last. A hiccup and a gaseous aftertaste scattered those thoughts.

"Stew still talking to you?" Jenks asked from near slumber.

"Yes," she answered, trying to rid her mouth of the caustic bitterness. "You never did tell me the type of meat."

"Sure did. Told you the name," he said. "And I would have bet money you wouldn't like eating dog." He rolled over and snored.

Her stomach churned. The stew's vapor erupted from her chest, singing through her nose. The thought of what she had gladly devoured earlier made her stand and head for the door. Her steps quickened as she grabbed the handle, flung it open, and charged out of the shack. When she reached the edge of the porch, her chest contracted, her puffed mouth exploded open, and her dinner piled up in the grass. She coughed several times, gained breath, then spat out the remainder.

"Guess he told you what was in the stew."

She looked at Cole's silhouetted figure standing at the end of the porch. She was too embarrassed to say anything.

"Took me that way too the first time I ate it. It takes a while to get used to." He threw her the shirt she had worn before. "I won't have need for that no more."

She took the garment and wiped her face. "Thank you." He stepped off the porch. "Clay," she said quickly, to stop him. "Thank you for everything. For saving my life and for being a friend to me."

He took a long time to reply. "Like I said, that's what I'm here for." He stepped back on the porch and walked toward her. As he stood next to her, she put her head to his chest. His arms wrapped around her back. His firm hold served the same sanctuary as it had the night before. She wanted to, but couldn't allow herself to put her arms around him for fear of falsely enticing his affections.

"Are you ever scared?" she asked, still feeling a little dizzy from being sick.

"Lots of times."

"Do you ever want someone just to talk to?" Her head sank against his warm chest.

"On occasion."

Numbness tingled through her body. "Well, if you ever need . . ." She was overwhelmed with drowsiness.

Chapter Ten

Claire awoke to a rancid smell. She squinted into the morning light shining through the broken window. The wool blanket was carefully spread over her. She pulled it around herself to fight the morning chill as she sat up. Jenks squatted in front of a small fire, stirring the contents of the pot.

"Morning."

Jenks looked grouchy. "Yup. Been that way for some time now."

She laughed to herself. The unmistakable smell of the previous night's stew hung in the air. "Is that from last night?"

Jenks nodded.

"For breakfast?"

"Yup. Dinner and supper too. Enough for the next three days in there."

She discarded his remark, noticing Cole's absence. "Where's Clay?"

"Outside."

"Doing what?"

"You just have to know everything, don't you? I never seen a woman that didn't want to know about things she didn't need to know."

"I just asked where he was. I hardly think it an unreasonable question."

Jenks shook his head disgustedly, stirring the stew as if churning butter. "He's seeing to the horses, I s'pose. Said he wanted to leave at first light, but I told him he need to be eatin' before." He took the rinsed plates from the table and ladled out two servings.

She rubbed the last bit of sleep from her eyes and sat at the table. The stew, left overnight, now had a putrid odor, but she took a bite and smiled graciously at Jenks. The nausea returned.

The door sprang open, flooding the cabin with sunlight. Cole stood in the doorway, his hand still on the handle, his brow creased. "Riders," he said, "heading this way."

Jenks's chair hit the floor as he ran outside. Claire followed both men to the front of the cabin. The sun hadn't yet crested the distant hills, leaving the adjacent cliffs in a shaded light. The men stood rigid, concentrating on something, while she scanned the rocks. She felt abandoned, unable to spot what it was they saw.

"I don't see a thing." Frustration laced her voice. "There's nothing moving out there."

Cole spoke in a monotone. "Don't look for what's moving. Look for what's not. Then you'll see it."

She tried again to see something, anything, but failed. "I still don't see it."

"I do," Jenks said. "Only one people rides that close in a single-file line." He turned to Cole. "What them Bluecoats doing up here?"

Claire finally found what they saw. Small dark figures, all in a long line miles away, moving in and out of the cover of the trees. It was such a great distance that she couldn't see them as men, much less soldiers, but she trusted what Jenks said to be true.

A loud sigh came from Cole and she looked at him. He glanced at her, then turned back toward the cabin. "Time to go."

She trailed the men back to the cabin. The saddled horses were reined to a tree. Cole immediately untied the Appaloosa's reins and began to mount, but stopped. He walked around to the roan and held out his hand.

Claire stood, surprised that he would remember to help her on her horse. She grinned in amazement.

"Come on," he ordered. Quickly, he lifted her onto the horse. She straightened her long skirt around the saddle. He mounted the Appaloosa, then swung around to face Jenks. "You comin' with us?"

"You know where I stays. I don't fear them none."

"Suit yourself."

"Wait, damn ya. Will take them an hour or more to get here," Jenks said, in his usual grouchy manner. "Don't even know where you're goin'."

"Well, tell me."

"First I got something for you." The black man hobbled back into the cabin, and after a loud crack, came back outside with a small canvas sack. "Here, take this. Been saving it a while." Cole caught the thrown sack. "It's some dried pig meat. You can eat it while you ride. Don't look like she's used to missing many meals."

Claire again was amazed by Jenks's kindness. For all his gruff manner, she detected that he liked her. She thanked him.

A twitch of his mouth was all the emotion he would show.

"All right," Cole interrupted. "Where do we go?"

"Follow the stream down the back till it meets up with the river. 'Fore long, you see it gettin' wider and the ground raise up to the cliffs. Keep sight of the water till you can hear it run over the rocks, then head west 'bout a mile or so. You see it. It's a big place. Take you the rest of the morning to get there."

Cole nodded, then his eyes softened. "You going to be okay?"

"Don't mind me none. I've been living here a long time, seen a lot, been through a lot. Them Bluecoats ain't after me. You just worry about getting her to her own."

Cole nudged his mount. "When I come back through, we'll finish that jug."

"Have it waiting on you."

Claire slowly waved her hand at the old black man as she followed Cole. Jenks raised his hand, then began rubbing it with the other in a vain attempt to hide his feelings.

The sun was high overhead as they rode up the hills that lined the river. Claire wiped the sweat from her brow with her sleeve, following the silent Cole—one of the few things she had become accustomed to on this trip. She was tired of the subservient role: always being told what to do, what not to do, and the like. She had heard which way the mine was, and she was going to get there as fast as possible. She kicked the roan to a gallop, but it reared up, and she was thrown to the ground. Rubbing her bruised backside, she spit the dirt from her lips. "Blast it."

"What did you do a fool thing like that for? You don't know this animal. You could've gone over the cliff there, or been carried for miles, locked in the stirrup."

She closed one eye to squint up at him, holding the retrieved mount by the bridle. She had indeed made a fool of herself and she didn't want to be reprimanded for it. "I wanted to get to John's mine as fast I could. How was I to know that this horse was so sensitive?"

Cole swung his head in disgust.

She understood his reaction, but she wouldn't apologize for her action. "I thought it would be you who would want to travel quickly. After all, aren't you fleeing the soldiers that were coming?" Her retort brought a change to his face, one that resembled the pain from a lash. "You're some kind of criminal or outlaw. That's why they're after you, isn't it?"

His stare told her she had learned something about him; she wasn't sure she wanted to pursue it if it meant facing any further wrath. But when he turned his head, she knew she had cut a nerve in him.

"Is that what you think?"

"Is it true?" she asked nervously, still eager for the answer.

"Depends on who's telling the story."

"I'm asking you. What is the truth, Clay?"

He dipped his chin to his chest for a moment, then with a deep breath dismounted. "This is as good a spot as any for a rest." He knelt and pulled the canvas sack from his pocket for a chunk of the meat, then tossed it to her. She opened the sack, took one of the chunks out, carefully placing the piece in her mouth. Although she was hungry, she sucked the salt from it first.

"I remember it being cold that morning. One of the coldest summer mornings I had ever known. I had been paid to scout for the Seventh Cavalry, under General Terry at the time. We was scouting most of the Dakota Territory, looking for the 'hostiles.' That's what they called them that wouldn't go to the reservation. Didn't make a damn to the army, or Washington, that these people had lived there for a hundred years and back. They just wanted them off the land that had gold on it, so white people could settle it. I went with them. I knew the land from my buffalo-hunting days, and there was good money to be made, thirty dollars in gold a month; it sure beat leading cattle drives from Texas."

She detected the somber attitude in his speech. The heat no longer affected her. Her entire attention was locked into his confession.

"I met up with Custer in the early summer. He was a strange one. He could be laughing one minute and barking orders at some other officer the next. You could feel that most around him didn't care for him. But me he didn't give no trouble. First day I met him, he give me one of the army issue pistols, Colt .45, brand new. I remember that day well," he recounted, while drawing the named revolver, holding the butt up to show her the 7 CAV stamping.

"But the others, they didn't like him. Fact is, most hated him. See, Custer got the taste for glory from the war. He saw what it done for President Grant, and he saw leading armies against the Lakota Sioux as a way of getting himself elected President. Nothing was going to stop him from that. You could see that in the way he walked, strutting around like a rooster. So, the time came for him to get his glory, to prove himself a great leader."

Cole took a deep breath, enough of a break for him to reach into the sack for another bite of the meat. Claire sensed his pause as a sign of the pain that Jenks had told of. His words came at a slow pace, as if tolled from a lonesome bell.

"Long about late June, Custer called out orders to move. We had known that Sitting Bull had called his people to camp with the Cheyenne, near the Little Bighorn river. The first orders were for us to join up with Colonel Gibbon and trap them all there, but Custer wanted to be there first. There weren't no glory in being part of the fight. He wanted to lead it. All the Indian scouts had told of a great group of tribes in the direction where we was heading, but Custer ignored all the reports.

"That second day I was given a sealed letter. Didn't expect one, but a special detail had brought information from General Terry. I remember the captain that gave me the paper. He

A SPECIAL OFFER
FOR LEISURE WESTERN
READERS ONLY!

Get FOUR FREE
Western Novels

Travel to the Old West in all its glory
and drama—without leaving your home!

Plus, you'll save between $3.00 and $6.00
every time you buy!

EXPERIENCE THE ADVENTURE AND THE DRAMA OF THE OLD WEST WITH THE GREATEST WESTERNS ON THE MARKET TODAY...FROM LEISURE BOOKS

As a home subscriber to the Leisure Western Book Club, you'll enjoy the most exciting new voices of the Old West, plus classic works by the masters in new paperback editions. Every month Leisure Books brings you the best in Western fiction, from Spur-Award-winning, quality authors. Upcoming book club releases include new-to-paperback novels by such great writers as:

Max Brand   Robert J. Conley   Gary McCarthy   Judy Alter
Frank Roderus   Douglas Savage   G. Clifton Wisler
David Robbins   Douglas Hirt

as well as long out-of-print classics by legendary authors like:

Will Henry   T. V. Olsen   Gordon D. Shirreffs

 Each Leisure Western breathes life into the cowboys, the gunfighters, the homesteaders, the mountain men and the Indians who fought to survive in the vast frontier. Discover for yourself the excitement, the power and the beauty that have been enthralling readers each and every month.

SAVE BETWEEN $3.00 AND $6.00 EACH TIME YOU BUY!

Each month, the Leisure Western Book Club brings you four terrific titles from Leisure Books, America's leading publisher of Western fiction. EACH PACKAGE WILL SAVE YOU BETWEEN $3.00 AND $6.00 FROM THE BOOKSTORE PRICE! And you'll never miss a new title with our convenient home delivery service.

 Here's how it works. Each package will carry a FREE 10-DAY EXAMINATION privilege. At the end of that time, if you decide to keep your books, simply pay the low invoice price of $13.44, no shipping or handling charges added. HOME DELIVERY IS ALWAYS FREE. With this price it's like getting one book free every month.

AND YOUR FIRST FOUR-BOOK SHIPMENT IS TOTALLY FREE!
IT'S A BARGAIN YOU CAN'T BEAT!

LEISURE BOOKS A Division of Dorchester Publishing Co., Inc.

GET YOUR 4 FREE BOOKS NOW—
A VALUE BETWEEN $16 AND $20

Mail the Free Book Certificate Today!

FREE BOOKS CERTIFICATE!

YES! I want to subscribe to the Leisure Western Book Club. Please send my 4 FREE BOOKS. Then, each month, I'll receive the four newest Leisure Western Selections to preview FREE for 10 days. If I decide to keep them, I will pay the Special Members Only discounted price of just $3.36 each, a total of $13.44. This saves me between $3 and $6 off the bookstore price. There are no shipping, handling or other charges. There is no minimum number of books I must buy and I may cancel the program at any time. In any case, the 4 FREE BOOKS are mine to keep—at a value of between $17 and $20! Offer valid only in the USA.

Name_____

Address_____

City_____ State_____

Zip_____ Phone_____

Biggest Savings Offer!

For those of you who would like to pay us in advance by check or credit card—we've got an even bigger savings in mind. Interested? Check here. ☐

If under 18, parent or guardian must sign.
Terms, prices and conditions subject to change. Subscription subject to acceptance. Leisure Books reserves the right to reject any order or cancel any subscription.

GET FOUR BOOKS TOTALLY *FREE*—A VALUE BETWEEN $16 AND $20

▼ Tear here and mail your FREE book card today! ▼

PLEASE RUSH
MY FOUR FREE
BOOKS TO ME
RIGHT AWAY!

Leisure Western Book Club
P.O. Box 6613
Edison, NJ 08818-6613

AFFIX
STAMP
HERE

and I had known each other when I was a trooper. But at that time, he didn't care for me none. I could tell by the face he gave me. Don't know why, except maybe 'cause I was making more money than he was and he was in the regular army, or something else—I don't know. Anyway, the letter was orders, at least I took it that way. The man sending it was a real powerful man, like your father. Only he had a lot more folks to worry about. I owed him. He didn't want any battle, any further war. He wanted peace between the Lakota and the whites, and he thought I might be able to get Sitting Bull to listen. I had once talked to the chief years back, before the treaty was made, in the Black Hills. But since the army broke it, I didn't think any of the Lakota would listen, not then. But I was told to try with only one thing made clear—I couldn't tell where I was going or what I was to do, and I couldn't tell of the man that had sent the letter. It wouldn't be good for a man like him to be making deals with the enemy. I understood the order."

Claire hugged her knees to her chest, entranced by every word.

"So I left in the night and rode to the river, where I thought they'd be. But soon as I got there, I got took by a Cheyenne scout party. They kept me away from Sitting Bull and I guess I was damned lucky not to have my throat cut. They didn't know who I was, but a white man dressed as one of them told the rest that killing a white man at that time would mean bad luck. All that man told me was that his name was Jon, and that he couldn't bring himself to kill a white man. But I was tied to a tree just across the river. I kept yelling so much about needing to talk to the chief, Jon stuffed my mouth with a rock. The Cheyenne kept me there in the camp for two days. Then came that cold morning."

He slowly swallowed, as if choking down the mentioned rock. Claire knew the memory pained him.

"Everyone came out of the lodges, the bucks mounting to ride out. Some said the *wasichu*, the whites, had come. There was craziness in the camp then. It was shortly after that I saw the dust rise over the hills and I knew that Custer was close. Sure enough, I was sitting right on the water's edge, watching. The soldiers came over the hill into the valley, charging at the camp. But those bucks who had left before now had returned. Hundreds of them, swarming like bees. Most of them that I could see had repeaters . . . just firing as fast as they could at the soldiers. Custer fell back, farther and farther. All they had were Springfields, which weren't no good in a close fight. Hell, they weren't even carrying no sabres. I just remember seeing those in blue and buckskin keep falling and falling, till there were too many Lakota to see any of them of the Seventh. It was about an hour, maybe longer, when the war cries stopped. Some of the young bucks came riding back to the camp, wearing army hats, shirts, and pants, carrying the Springfields over their heads as a sign of victory. That's when I knew it was over."

Claire sat motionless. She could feel the sorrow in his voice as he described the battle. When he stopped, she still hadn't learned all she wanted to know. "How did you survive?"

He grinned at her question. "That was my curse. Jon came at me with a knife when it was over. At first I thought he meant to cut me open, but he cut me loose from the tree instead, and pulled the rock from my mouth. He told me to go and look at the whites, at the soldiers. That if I wanted peace, to go tell the whites more soldiers would die, like those of the Seventh, if more came. They gave me my horse and I rode out from the camp, real slow, so none of them would think me running to get help. But they let me ride. Some of them watched, but none followed. When I got to the top of the rise, that's when I saw what they wanted me to see. Men and horses scattered in the grass, all dead. Most of the troopers naked. Blood covered the bodies; arrows stuck in them; they'd been scalped, heads and arms lopped off."

Cole swallowed hard again, straining to keep talking.

"I went down to where they lay. I could see the wounds still pumping blood out of some of them. Then I saw Colonel Custer. He'd been stripped too, but he still had his scalp. A bullet hole in his chest looked like the shot went through his heart. Like most of them, he looked like he died at the start of it, and the fight was over real quick. Glory killed him, it killed him and the rest. I sat down in the grass next to the men I had known that short time. I don't know how long I sat there. That's all I remember of that day. Twenty-five June, eighteen and seventy-six."

"Why does the army want you? There was nothing you could have done. You did nothing wrong."

"They didn't see it that way. The next morning I rode to where I thought General Terry was. I stopped when I saw some of the Indian scouts that I knew were with the Seventh. I heard their stories of what went on. It wasn't till I was about to leave that one of them told me the army was wanting me. They said it was being said that I left the troops to go to Sitting Bull and warn him of the attack. I thought the story was a lie until I got to the perimeter of General Terry's camp. Sentries recognized me, telling me to halt and surrender, then they started firing at me. That's when I knew as a fact I was being considered a traitor. *Collaborator* they called it. I did the only thing I could think of at the time. I ran. Been running since."

"But the message. You could have shown the message you were given."

"It said in the letter that I couldn't tell who

sent me or why I was sent. It would have to be denied. A man running the country couldn't be—"

"President Grant?" Claire gasped loudly.

Cole's look of anger at himself acknowledged her guess. "That's two of us now."

"But what of the man who gave you the letter? He must have known."

"No," Cole said, shaking his head. "He never knew what was in it. It was sealed. Although I have heard that he, more than most, wants to stand me in front of a wall."

"How do you know this?"

"I know him. Heard he made major after the Little Bighorn. Guess they needed more ranking officers then. I heard that he had been put in charge of my capture, volunteered for it, as a matter of fact. What I know of him since, sounds like he wants to be the next army hero."

"What's his name?" Claire asked.

"Perry. Miles Perry."

Sparks flared the end of the wood. Jenks moved the matchstick over his pipe and sucked the fire down the bowl. Smoke spiraled into the mild breeze. His weight on the rocker's old rungs forced a long aching creak. He shaved off the splinters from the carved wooden pony in his hands. Clouds had drifted over the mountain, blocking the sunshine from the cabin, cutting the glare from the faces of the soldiers lining up in a long row in front of him. He folded the whittle knife closed.

"Good afternoon," said the bearded officer at the head of the row. "I'm Major Perry and this is Lieutenant Moore." His face was steel cold. "I'm looking for a man."

Jenks gave a puzzled look at the line of soldiers. "Thems you got no good?"

Perry's face didn't crack at the remark. "The man I'm looking for is named Cole. Tall, about six foot six. A man of thirty by now. I have reason to believe that he passed through here and may be traveling with a woman he's kidnapped. Have you seen such a man?"

"What do you want him for?"

"That's army business. This man Cole is dangerous. I've personally seen six men that he's killed while following him here. I fear the woman might be next. Now, have you seen this man?"

Jenks couldn't avoid the question, but Cole needed another two hours to get to the mine. He had to keep the troopers off the trail as long as he could. "No," he answered, shaking his head quickly. "I ain't seen nobody like that."

Perry sat motionless for a moment, then turned his head toward the side of the cabin, where hoofprints were chopped out of the wet soil. "Who was here before us?"

Jenks looked at the prints, drew deeply on the pipe, snorting the smoke. "Them's from two

Mex came through early this morning, heading for town."

"We've just come from there. I didn't see any men riding to town. Why would they travel up the mountain to get there?"

"I can't say. Why don't you ask them that? You can catch 'em if you hurry."

Perry shook his head slowly "No, I don't think I'll do that." The major's face told Jenks that his tale wasn't going to help him or Cole.

"You wouldn't be lying to us, would you, boy?" grunted one of the troopers.

Jenks stared at the soldier who made the remark. "I don't know who you're talking to, seein' that I was here when there weren't no army. Killing Injuns and cutting paths while your mama was wiping the yellow off your white butt."

The angered trooper put his hand on his holstered revolver.

"Sergeant Lewis," Lieutenant Moore shouted. "We are soldiers of the United States. Not the Confederacy."

"Yes, that's right, Sergeant," Perry concurred, with the sincerity of a snake, keeping his eyes firmly on the old man. "So I'm sure our host here wouldn't mind cooling our tempers with a drink of water. Sergeant, see what's in the house."

Lewis motioned to another trooper and both men dismounted, drew their side arms, and cautiously stepped by Jenks to enter the cabin.

135

Metal crashing and wood cracking came from inside, and then the two emerged.

"There's nothing in there but a stinking pot," Lewis reported.

Jenks scowled at the opinion of the stew.

"Take some men and secure the perimeter. I believe there's something here he's forgotten to tell us," Perry ordered. The entire troop fanned out around the cabin. "What is your name?"

"Jenks. My name's Jenks."

"Well, Mr. Jenks, aiding a traitor is a capital crime. Dealt with harshly." He squeezed the rein ends tightly, forming a loop at the end, slapping it in his palm.

Jenks sat undisturbed. "Won't be the first time a white man tried to show me how powerful he is with something in his hand. You could ask them who tried, but they all dead now."

"Major, sir," Moore whispered. "I must remind you that this isn't why we were sent here."

Perry turned to the young lieutenant. "I tire of your questioning my actions. If you've not the stomach to be a leader of men, Moore, then I suggest you resign your rank and take up more placid pursuits. I'm trying to track down an enemy of the army. You're more concerned with being paid."

"Major Perry," called out a soldier galloping up from behind the cabin. "There's two graves about one hundred yards from here. The dirt looks freshly dug, sir."

Jenks closed his eyes for a moment, knowing what the discovery meant to his fate.

A satisfied grin took over Perry's face. "Lieutenant Moore. Take six of the men and proceed to meet the payroll rendezvous. Express my apologies to Major Parker for not being there personally. Tell him I had more urgent duty here."

Chapter Eleven

"Why don't you surrender?" Claire asked. She walked next to Cole as they both led their horses up the hill. "It would seem the right thing to do to clear your name."

"Oh, I thought about it, more than once. But every time I come within sight of an army post, I can't help but change my mind."

"You don't think you'd get a fair trial?"

Cole shook his head. "It wouldn't be no trial with a judge and a jury. It'd be a court-martial, with generals sitting at a table. The army don't concern itself with being fair. It's just concerned with getting the results it wants."

"Surely President Grant would see to your acquittal. After all, you said he wrote you the message."

"A man such as him can't get in a mess such as mine. I knew what it would do to him if it was known that he'd sent the letter. Years back, I was with my pa when he got killed in the war. The gen—the president knew my pa. It was him that took hold of me, got me in the army, gave me something to live for after my pa died. He became like a pa to me. I couldn't drag him down just to save my own skin."

She stopped walking, forcing him to as well. "Then you'll go on running? Until they catch you or kill you?"

His face drew long and his eyes penetrated into hers. "What would that be to you?"

The curt remark sank her heart, drawing the breath from her body. She stared blankly as he walked back to the Appaloosa and threw the stirrup over the saddle to tighten the cinch. She was unable to move toward him, until a smirk came over his face.

"Anyway, knowing that man has brought me work. That reminds me, you have a mid name? One other than Claire?"

The question pulled her from the sorrow. Her mind began wondering as to the reason for his inquiry. "Yes. Why do you ask?"

"I just need to know. What is it?"

All at once it became clear. The mystery of this man's presence in her life made sense.

From the very start at Platte Falls—his rough manner toward her, the hardship he'd proclaimed would beset her life since her arrival, his discouragement of her continuing on to join John at the mine. These actions could only have come from the orders of one man. "You bastard!"

Cole's head sprang up to see her raging eyes. "Huh?"

"Yes, I do have a middle name," she raged, strutting up to him. "And there's only one reason for you to know to ask."

Now Cole looked bewildered as he gazed at the ire in her face.

"The name you're looking for is George. My given name is Claire George Thorsberg. I was named that because it was my father's wish to have a son, and name that son after his own father, a family tradition. But he had a daughter, an only daughter. A shame put upon me since I was born. And now you ask me about it, a name only he, Jacob Thorsberg, would know about."

Cole pulled his arms in close to his sides, palms out. "I can see you don't brag on it much."

"All this time it was you acting as his agent to convince me to turn around and go back to Baltimore."

"Now wait. I was just doing a job that told me to take you to your husband. I don't know anything about your family or trying to make you turn back."

She contemplated his excuse a moment. "I don't believe you. What did my father do to get you to guide me here?"

Cole took a deep breath, his eyes wandering from hers as a child would confess to a mother after being caught in a lie. "A letter found me on a mountain in the Nevada desert. The only man who knew I was there and could get it to me was Sam Grant. It said to be in Platte Falls on the first of August. To meet a woman and provide escort, to bring her to her husband at a silver mine in the hills."

Claire listened to his story, careful not to let her resolve soften. "Go on."

"It said to wire by the fifth that she had met her husband with proof being her mid name."

"And?"

"To wait for a wire at the nearest Wells-Fargo for the reward."

"And what was that to be?"

"One thousand dollars," he answered, throwing the stirrup off the saddle.

She weighed what he had said, nodding her head. "So was this easier than driving cattle from Texas?"

"No."

"Harder, I suppose."

"Didn't think it'd be." His voice grew firm. "But cattle don't squarrel near as loud."

"So you feel you've earned your money?"

"Every penny."

Her mouth fell, then snapped shut. "Well, I will not be nursemaided by a nanny in boots. I hereby relieve you of your obligation, Mr. Clay Cole. You have done your job. You may go back to Platte Falls and claim your fee. I will go on alone from here." She stepped into the stirrup quickly, not allowing him a chance to help her.

"That damn pride of yours. You wear it like a badge."

"And you see it as a stain."

He paused before answering her. "Well, Mrs. Rhodes, I won't do that."

"And why is that? You're going to tell me that you can't conscience leaving a woman alone here? Even one that 'squarrels' worse than cattle?"

"No," he answered honestly. "It's just that there is no Fargo office in Platte Falls. The nearest that I know of is in a town called Nobility. About a hundred miles or better in this direction. So it seems we'll still share the same path." His grin boiled her stomach. She took her anger out on the roan's flanks and galloped off.

Claire gripped the reins tightly, watching for signs of the trail leading to the mine despite the beauty of the majestic snowcaps, a distraction she found hard to ignore. She'd followed the turns of the river for about an hour and now headed away from it to the west. She approached a slope that grew larger with every stride of the roan. The slope gave way to a gully. Tree stumps dotted a line separating it from the surrounding forest. She felt close. She kicked the roan, and the horse was quickly at a gallop. Air blew against her face and through her hair with the speed. Her heart beat rapidly in anticipation of reaching her destination and John's loving embrace. Cole came riding up from behind and grabbed the bridle of the roan, rearing it to a stop.

"Let my horse go. I can see it."

"Wait," Cole ordered. "This isn't a church social. You're likely to be shot off that horse, barging in like that."

"And what would that be to you? You will still have earned your money."

He paused a moment, then released his grip on the bridle. "All right. Go get your head shot off."

She nudged her mount to a slow walk and came to the edge of the gully. A gaping hole in the side of a rock wall was supported by large, chiseled beams. Rails ran from the mouth down the gully, ending at a small plateau, where a teamless wagon waited below. She searched for John, but saw only a stranger in a black leather vest standing on the porch of a small shack, his hand propped on his holstered pistol. This was not what she had envisioned, but she wouldn't let her disappointment show to the approaching Cole.

"Pardon me," she called to the man. "Where is John Rhodes?"

The man entered the shack and closed the door. Cole's face was drawn. His hand slipped to his .45.

"What is it? Something else doesn't meet with your approval?"

He nodded. "Nobody's digging."

The shack door opened and out walked a hatless man with a welcoming smile. He was dressed in a white tailored shirt covered by a shimmering vest and a string tie. The long black pants stretched over his black boots as he came toward them, his walk steadied by the use of a cane. The man with the black leather vest stepped back on the porch.

"Is that your husband?" Cole whispered.

Claire shook her head.

"How do you do? Are you Claire?" She returned his smile and dismounted to take the man's outstretched hand.

"Yes, I am. And you are?"

"Hoyt Larsen is my name. I feel like I know you from what all John has told me."

"Where is he?"

"He's down in the shaft."

Claire started for it, but Larsen stopped her.

"You can't go down there. It's much too dangerous for a dainty thing such as yourself."

"But I can't wait. Will you go and get him? No, I want it to be a surprise. Oh, I don't know what to do." She brought her hand over her mouth, while thinking of how she should meet her husband.

"Well, maybe your friend would go and get him," said Larsen.

"No," Claire answered quickly.

"I'm sure a man like him knows how to be careful." Larsen walked up to the Appaloosa. "Pleased to meet you. I'm Hoyt Larsen," he said, offering a handshake.

Cole didn't return the gesture.

"I don't care to be friendly with you," Cole said coldly.

Larsen slowly dropped his hand to his side.

"You sent two of your gunnies to run a friend of mine off his place. They damn near killed Mrs. Rhodes."

Larsen looked confused. "What? I didn't— who were these men? They worked for me?"

"Yes," Claire said. "There is that matter. It was horrible. But I'm sure it can all be explained. Please, forgive his rudeness. I promised I would discuss it with John. Now I want to see my husband."

Larsen looked at her, then peered over his shoulder.

Claire watched his face and followed his movement. At the corner of the shaft opening stood a man. He too was dressed in a white tailored shirt and black trousers, but without a vest or tie. His black hair was combed back from his young face. He propped himself against one of the beams.

She took a step, then another, and ran toward her husband. She flew into his arms. He didn't hug her as lovingly as she had hoped. She wiped at her tearing eyes while peering into his, trying hard not to cry in public, failing to suppress a childish giggle, unable to think of what to say at that moment. It had been a year, and she had forgotten how sometimes his expression wouldn't reflect hers. She wrapped her arms around his neck, pressing her cheek to his. "Oh, I love you. I missed you so much. Can you believe I'm here?"

"No." The surprise in his voice sounded genuine. She looked back in his eyes and was about to kiss him, but thought it better to save that kind of welcome for when they were alone.

"It's been such a long time. There were times when I thought I would never see you again. Some of them occurred just getting here from the train."

He looked past her, concentrating on the others.

"I guess I should say hello and thank your companion," he said, putting weight on weak legs, slightly stumbling.

She noticed his labored effort to balance himself. "It's gotten worse since you left Baltimore."

He didn't respond, but made his way to where Larsen and Cole were.

She followed, her hand touching his arm for moral support.

"I guess I owe you a debt of gratitude for seeing my wife safely here," he said, as he offered his hand up to Cole. "I'm John Rhodes."

"Clay Cole. My pleasure."

"My wife tells me you had some trouble on the way."

Cole nodded. "Some. But we made it."

"Well, what's the saying?—'That's why they call it Danger Ridge,'" Larsen remarked.

Cole cocked his head, looking toward the shack.

Claire looked too, but no one was standing there now.

"Is there something wrong?" Larsen asked.

Cole took a long breath. "No. Just I'm not used to seeing miners dressed in leather and sportin' hoglegs."

Rhodes and Larsen each broke into a grin.

"Well, you can't be too careful up here. My wife will come to know this. A man has to protect what is his. Whether it's his land or his property."

Cole looked back at Claire. "Or his pretty wife."

Her eyes met his, then she lowered her head.

"Could we offer you a drink to wash out the dust?" Larsen asked.

Both of the Rhodeses looked surprised at him for making the kindly offer.

"No," Claire firmly answered. "Mr. Cole has other business to tend to, and I'm sure he wants to see to it as soon as possible."

Cole nodded. "Mrs. Rhodes is right. I do have other business."

She took two small steps toward Cole and offered him her hand. "Thank you for everything. I hope you collect your fee promptly. Good-bye, Mr. Cole."

He wiped his palm on his pantleg and took her hand.

She kept looking at his shirt, while sensing his stare on her face.

He reined in, turning his horse. Looking back, he caught her eyes once more and tipped his hat brim.

She looked away. The beating hooves faded within seconds.

Chapter Twelve

Claire stepped into the mine shack. Her first impression was of what she'd seen in Jenks's cabin; mud-masoned walls of timber, planked floor, but no windows. There was at least a pot-bellied stove, but it would take a long time to make this house into a woman's home.

John followed her inside. She turned and approached him slowly, feeling awkward about sharing the first moment alone with her husband in nearly a year. She took his free hand and came closer. He seemed indifferent to her advances. She thought to kiss him, but didn't. She released his hand when Larsen entered. Her affection would have to wait.

John looked toward Larsen as he left the door

open a crack for a moment, then closed it. "Is he gone?" John asked him.

A quick nod was the reply.

John turned to face her.

She stared into his gray, loveless eyes. "Why did you have to come here?" he demanded.

"What do you mean?" she asked, her smile fading.

"Haven't you done enough to ruin my life?"

"John, what are you saying? I came to be with you. To start a new life with you here in the West." Her eyes searched for the love they once shared, but his reaction showed no signs of it. She hugged his chest. "John, oh sweet dear John. What has happened to you here that you treat me as an intruder? I wanted to be with you. To live here with you. To start a family here."

He slowly unwrapped her arms, then clutched her shoulders to push her back. "That time has past."

"It's not too late. We're both young, we'll have time—"

"No, Claire!" John's brow wrinkled. "This time you will have to listen to me. Had I known you were coming, I would have insisted you stay in Baltimore."

Claire stumbled back from the words. "John, I came here for you. I am your wife."

John paused as he glanced at the wall. "Who was that man?"

Claire took a deep breath. "He's just a man."

John's chin tightened.

"Father paid him—" She stopped as her words creased his brow further.

"Jacob? There's that name again. Why did you think I left Baltimore? To escape Jacob Thorsberg and the rest of your family, that's why. Every day I worked for that man he made it clear what he was, and what I wasn't." His face turned red.

"I know that. He didn't want me to come here either. But I did, for you. I love you, John."

His face showed resistance. A pause brought John's attention to her dress. "Where did you get that awful rag? It is hardly your fashion taste as I remember it."

Claire looked at the blouse and skirt, but thought first before answering. Her honesty had already stirred his anger. The truth might send him into a rage, but she didn't have any other explanation and she didn't lie well. "I had planned to arrive in a beautiful dress from Paris I bought while I was in New York. I'd hoped you would think it lovely, John." She paused, due to his scowl. "But it became soiled during the trip here."

"And where did you get that?"

"It was lent to me by a friend of Mr. Cole's."

"What?"

"Wasn't that mighty nice of him?" Larsen sniped.

Claire snapped around to him, and saw his smug grin.

John's receding scowl showed that he'd forgotten about Larsen's presence also. "Hoyt, will you excuse us? It has been a year since I've seen my wife."

"Of course. Forgive my manners," Larsen said, the smug grin still in place. "John, why don't you show your bride to the room in the back? I'll bunk in with the boys. We'll start on a place for the two of you tomorrow."

John nodded as if embarrassed. "Thank you, Hoyt."

Larsen gripped the cane and limped out of the cabin.

As the door shut, John turned to her.

She met his eyes. "I had hoped for a more loving welcome."

"There was a time I actually did love you. But you were too busy with your social friends. You were never my wife, Claire. You and Jacob were just alike. That's why I left. For as long as I stayed, I would always be the man who'd married Jacob Thorsberg's daughter. I had to have my own life."

"And I will always be his daughter. But I came out here because being your wife was more important to me."

"I don't want you here. Can't you understand that?"

His words stabbed her heart, bleeding the love from her soul. She fought back tears while looking at the man she'd risked her life to be with.

John stared at the wall. "I'm not the same man you married." He sighed. "Life here is harsh, Claire."

"I've seen that."

"No. You haven't. In order to survive in this land, I had to do things I'm not proud of," he said in an ominous voice.

"Such as?"

"I've gotten used to taking things, Claire. Things that weren't mine, but were there for the taking. Things I could take if I wanted them bad enough. And I did want them."

A chill streaked through her spine. "What are you telling me, John?"

He hesitated, his face dispirited as he looked deeply at her. Then a slight smirk cut across his face. "You must be tired from the trip."

"What were you going to tell me?"

"Later. It's a very long story."

He took her arm and guided her toward a door at the far corner of the room. He opened the door and another small, dust-filled room appeared. She entered to see a timber-framed bed centered to the far wall, where clothes hung above it.

Claire stood stunned by the idea that this was where she would have to live. The hardships she'd been told of, but had hoped weren't true, were now before her.

She sat on the sheetless mattress and collapsed in the middle, the stuffing inside no firmer then that of a cot.

John pulled her back to her feet. "You see what luxuries we have here. I'll bring in a pot and draw some water for you. That's as close as you'll get to a bath, until I can figure out how to get you to the river." He walked out the doorway and turned. "We normally eat about sundown." He closed the door.

She sank back down in the bed. All the while during the trip across the nation she had dreamed of a new life in a new country. She had ignored the warnings of what life would be at a mine. Now, despite her pride, she regretted her obstinacy. Besides being in a strange land with the man she had sworn to love for better or for worse, she was truly alone.

Night had fallen. Claire sat at the table with a bottle of whiskey and two glasses in the center. The room was lit by a single lantern hung in the center of the ceiling. She stared at the walls of the shack. Hoyt Larsen stirred dinner in a pot on the stove. It smelled familiar, and she wanted to talk.

"Is that beans?" she asked politely.

He turned with a smile. "Yes, it is. You have a good nose."

"I recognized the od—aroma."

John came inside, carrying a bucket of sloshing water and a porcelain basin.

"I had beans the first night I was here."

John stopped and frowned at her. "You'd better get used to it." He continued into the back room to place the water and basin, then sat next to her.

Larsen brought the steaming pot to the table and plopped a helping on her dish. She took notice of his labored walk, and Larsen saw her watching.

"Forgive me for staring, I'm sorry."

"No trouble. I deserve it for doing something as stupid as stepping off my horse wrong, right on top of a rock near a week ago. Twisted it good." He laughed. "Well, Claire, have you enjoyed your trip here?"

She hesistated a moment. "It certainly has been a unique experience."

"Just how unique?"

She smiled. "John, you know me. I've never done anything like this."

"Including traveling with a strange man for two days?"

Claire sensed the contempt in his voice. She stopped smiling.

"Do you know that man, Claire?" Larsen asked.

Not to sound like a fool, she nodded. "I met him at the train."

"Did you know about him, about his past, his reputation?"

"What are you getting at, Hoyt?" John asked.

"Nothing, John." He smiled and poured the whiskey in both glasses. "I was just talking with the boys. They say they've heard he was an army deserter."

"He's not a deserter, Mr. Larsen. He was wrongly accused of treason."

"Claire! Just how do you know this?"

"He told me. We did talk while we were coming here."

"What else did you do while coming here?" John slugged down the whiskey. Larsen quickly refilled the glass.

"I beg your pardon? I see no reason to ask me that. Clay was a complete gentleman."

"Clay? I see you did get to know him well."

"John, please," she whispered. "We needn't discuss such things in front of others. Let's change the subject." She turned to Larsen. "So, Mr. Larsen—"

"Please call me Hoyt."

"All right, Hoyt. How is the mining business?" John scoffed and swigged his whiskey again.

"We're doing fine, just fine. Why, we have one of the best mines in the state. And I have prospects on another one. I'm going to make your husband a rich man."

"Oh, and how is that?"

John pushed away his plate and brought the whiskey bottle in front of him to again refill his glass.

Larsen's grin grew even wider. "I know where the mine they call 'the Matchless' is."

"Matchless? Why is it called that?"

He let out a slight laugh as he rose from his chair and went to a shelf near the stove. He opened a wooden box, pulled out a cigar, and lit it. "Because none of the others come close. A vein of silver that stretches for miles."

A memory came to mind. "Rich in silver ore like no other? Someone has already found it."

Larsen's smile was gone.

John stopped drinking. "How did you know that?"

"I read it, in a newspaper."

"Where?"

"The newspaper? Jenks, a friend—"

"No, damn it. The mine. Where is the mine?" demanded John.

Claire sensed his angered tone and noticed an eager interest on Larsen's face. "I believe it was found near a town named Leadville, if I remember correctly."

John's head slumped to the table.

Larsen, his snide grin long gone, stared at his cigar, then took a long puff. "I'm sorry to hear that, Claire. I'm very sorry to hear that."

John rose and hobbled to the shelf, where he picked up a lantern. He lit it and passed by the table, grabbing the whiskey bottle on his way to the back room.

Claire sensed she had said something wrong, but she didn't know what, and feared asking. While Larsen continued staring at his cigar, she left the table and headed for the back room.

"Excuse me. I think I'll rest now," she said to Larsen.

"I'm real sorry you said that, Claire. Real sorry."

She walked into the back room, lit by the lantern which hung on the wall, and shut the door behind her. John lay on the bed, one arm over his eyes, while his other hand held the bottle.

John smelled of whiskey and seemed to have passed out from his drunkenness. She didn't want to disturb him.

The porcelain basin on the floor reflected the lantern's light, and she noticed her own odor.

She crept up to the basin and dipped her hand in the water. She patted her face. Rolling up the sleeves of her blouse, she wiped her arms, then her neck. She unbuttoned the blouse front and continued wetting her skin. At last, she removed her blouse and skirt and squatted next to the basin. She spread the water under her camisole and all over her body until she felt as clean as possible under the limitations.

When she stood, hands gripped her waist, and she was forced back onto the bed. John pounced on top of her, his hand covering her mouth.

Her heart raced when she saw his crazed eyes.

"Did you like being with your friend, Claire? Did you enjoy being with a wanted man?" He kissed her neck and the front of her chest. "How would you like to be with me? Your husband. Or did you forget you had one?" He knelt on the bed and quickly pulled off his trousers. He removed his hand and mashed his lips to hers.

His liquored stench was glazed over her face.

She pushed futilely against him. She raised her knee, striking his thigh, forcing him back.

"John, please no," she shrieked.

He pushed his hand over her mouth again, and with the other he clenched his fist, took heavy breaths, then gripped the cloth of her pantaloons. She soon felt the cool air surround her bare skin. He lay back on top of her and whispered, "I'm a murderer."

She tried to breathe, but couldn't from the terror seizing her chest. A moment later, he was inside her. The pain tore not only at her inner flesh, but at her soul as well. What seemed hours of torment was over in seconds. John groaned and slowly collapsed next to her. His hand slipped from her mouth. Soon, his occasional strained breathing meant he had again fallen asleep.

The most horrible minutes of her life were over. She kept her eyes closed, the agony she felt throughout her body and heart dripped as tears into the unsheeted mattress. She didn't know who John Rhodes was anymore. This wasn't the man she'd married. He would never have done this to her. And had he really killed someone? She couldn't live with that thought.

The pain of admitting the mistake she had made in coming West was incomparable to the indignity she had just endured. In that instant, her decision was made. She was leaving, that night.

She waited until she was sure he was soundly

asleep, then she eased out of the bed and slipped on her blouse and skirt. Taking the lantern off the wall, she opened the door only enough to squeeze through and gently close it.

She held up the lantern and headed for the outer door. How she would make her escape she wasn't sure, but her mind was made up. She passed the table, spotting the empty glasses and dishes, but also noticed a stack of what looked like paper. Closer inspection showed them to be some official documents with people's names. She didn't want to delay, but the light, rolling script across the top revealed one name she recognized, *Lucious Jenkins*.

She bent down to read the paper. It was a deed of property with Jenks's name, showing it as sold to Hoyt Larsen. She recalled what the old black man had said about being forced from his land, and here lay evidence. Perhaps John had planned to murder Jenks. She would have never believed it until now. Only if she acted quickly could she avert this terrible possibility.

Hoyt Larsen's voice shot through the room. "I'm sorry, did you lose something, Claire?" He stood in the open door, gripped his cane, and hobbled to the table. "Now, I'm really sorry." He took the stack of papers and waved them at Claire. "Do you see these?" These are land claims I bought, foreclosed on, and have taken over for the last two years. Soon I'll have the rest of them."

"And who owns that land? Do you?"

"Right now, a bunch of unorganized miners working small stakes just to risk their pitiful lives for a few sacks of ore. When I'm done taking over here, I'll be the richest man in the West."

"What about me, Hoyt?" John demanded from the back room door.

Claire turned and shone the light on him. He limped next to her.

"John, good of you to join us," said Larsen.

"Aren't you forgetting about me?"

"John, what is this?" Claire asked. "What have you done? I thought you came here to mine for silver."

A smirk creased Larsen's face. "Oh yes, when we started. But things didn't go as planned."

"Go ahead. Tell her the rest." John peered at Claire. "Tell her how we kept digging, but found nothing. So we dug deeper. When we hit water, you simply told the men to keep digging, that you'd give them interests in the mine, to just keep digging. Until the shaft flooded, and they were all killed."

"Shut up."

"No, I won't, Hoyt. I'm sick of this. I'm sick of the thought of what we did. My God, Hoyt, we murdered people just to get rich."

"Oh God," Claire exclaimed.

"Yes, I can say it. This mine has taken all of my money." He looked at Claire. "And part of my soul." He faced Larsen. "I'm not putting another dime in this nightmare."

161

Claire stared at her husband. "Why did you send the telegram?"

"What telegram? I never sent any telegram."

"No, but I did," Larsen said coldly, drawing a small Derringer pistol from his pocket and pointing it at both of them. "John was always mentioning how much money your family had."

"What?" John shouted. "You told her to come here?"

"I wired for her to send the money. She's the one who decided to come with it."

John closed his eyes and shook his head. "Why?"

"The Matchless. I've seen it. Chicken Bill Lovell showed it to me. It's mine for ten thousand dollars."

"Someone's found it. Didn't you hear her?"

"It's a lie."

"You idiot. Do you think he would just show it to you? He salted it with silver to take in fools like you."

"And the rest of the money? You were going to use it to buy more land?" Claire asked.

"Fifty thousand buys a lot of acres out here."

She dipped her head, knowing what a fool she'd been. She had done many things to be embarrassed for on this trip, but now she felt only shame. "My God, John. Tell me this isn't true."

He turned away from her.

"He never could make up his mind," Larsen said as he aimed the Derringer. "He had planned to end it for good with you some day. It seems that's been left to me." He cocked the hammer.

"No, Hoyt, wait," John called.

Larsen pointed the pistol at him. "Do you want to be next? We can't have her getting in the way. Hell, think of it, John. With the inheritance we might go on to California."

"No!" John screamed as he lunged in front of Claire. A loud blast rang out. John cringed and doubled over onto the floor.

"Oh my God! Oh my God!" Claire cried as John lay on his back. She knelt by him and moved his black hair away from his glazing eyes. Blood trickled from his mouth. His white shirt quickly turned red around the hole in his chest. "Oh no, John. Please don't leave me. Oh please, God. Help me."

John's blood-stained hand palmed her cheek. "I'm sorry, Claire," he gasped. "Claire, my wife, forgive me." His eyes rolled up. The eyelids blinked quickly, then stopped. His hand fell limp.

"Oh John," she wept, hugging his bloody chest.

"Do you see what trouble you've caused already?"

She wiped the tears away and saw the smirking Larsen aiming at her again.

She thought to close her eyes, but she couldn't. She coldly stared at him, thinking of the one thing that would stop him and save her life. "You can't get the money without me."

"You're bluffing."

"It's all drawn on a draft from the Bank of Baltimore. It's worthless without my signature."

The smirk fell from his face. "It's not true."

"Do you think me careless enough to bring fifty thousand dollars in cash?"

The pistol's aim slowly lowered to the floor. "Damn you to hell, lady."

The outer door flung open, flooding the shack with the morning light. Another man came running in. He looked first at Larsen, then at Claire, kneeling over John's body.

After a moment's thought, Larsen limped over and grabbed her arm, yanking her off the floor. "Ed, get the horses," he yelled. "We're going to Platte Falls."

After a sleepless night and a cold supper, Cole started riding back toward Jenks's cabin, ever on the lookout for any of the soldiers he knew would be there by now. It had been a long time since he'd seen anybody that might be on his trail, and he had a mind to turn and head to Nobility to collect the money he was owed. However, he wanted to see that Jenks hadn't run into trouble with the army. No sense causing that old man grief because of him.

Still, there was something gnawing at him. Things didn't seem right when he left. The gunman at the cabin, the lack of miners present at the mine, and the way Rhodes acted in front of Claire, his wife, a woman he hadn't laid eyes on in a year.

But that was where the lady wanted to be, and since she was mad at Cole for working for her father, it wasn't his concern anymore.

One thing wouldn't leave his mind, something that Hoyt Larsen had said. He reined in the Appaloosa as the thought grew larger. How could Larsen have known they'd traveled through Danger Ridge? Cole had second thoughts himself about taking her that way. How could Larsen have been sure that was the way they had traveled? And if Cole himself had not taken her to the mine, how did Rhodes plan on her getting there?

He peered back toward the mine. It still was not his affair. He had done his job. But the gnawing wasn't going to leave his head until he knew something for sure. "Come on, Pepper," he said, turning the Appaloosa and spurring it to a gallop.

He reined in a short distance from the mine and dismounted. He tied the reins to a tree and cautiously approached through the brush. He just wanted to see if she was all right. One sight of her walking around would tell him that she had already started settling the place and he could be on his way.

He got to the top of the small rim which surrounded the mine, being careful not to be noticed. He'd rather Claire not know he was there watching her. Bobbing his head through the tangled branches, he caught a view from behind the shack's roof of the dirt path leading to the shaft. He didn't see anyone.

Loud voices began to rise out of the silence, then Claire appeared in front of the shack, with Larsen pulling her by the arm. They were arguing. When Claire resisted Larsen's repeated yanks, he knew she was in trouble. Larsen revealed a gun, pointed at Claire, and Cole reached for his Colt, only to stop at the ratchet of a hammer breaking the silence behind his own head.

"I've been praying for the day I'd get the drop on you," whispered a familiar voice.

Cole closed his eyes and put a face to the voice.

"I knew you wouldn't be far away from your brother," he said, slowly turning to see the red-haired Carl Hensley pointing a .44 at him.

"Now I can plug his back-shooting killer. I heard about what really happened in Platte Falls."

"That weren't all my fault. He turned tail too fast for me to get in front of him."

"Shut up about Caleb. Throw your gun and the knife here, easy like."

Cole slowly pulled the weapons free and tossed them at Hensley's feet.

"Hey, boys. Come look what I found me."

Three men quickly ran out of the brush and

stood next to Hensley, pointing their side arms at Cole.

"Now you watch him. He's real quick. I got to go tell the boss man about this. I guess we'll have need of two graves now."

The men laughed.

Cole's jaw tightened, a sight Hensley seemed to enjoy.

"Maybe as a bonus, the boss may let us all have a poke at that gal you brought."

Cole didn't react to the remark.

"How is it? Or were you not man enough to find out? If you're a good boy, I might let you watch us with her before I kill you."

The men laughed louder.

"Careful, Carl, she's a mean one."

"I've had tougher than her."

"Yeah, but she's tough to please. She has high ex-pects. Talk used to be that those you didn't pay couldn't keep from giggling."

The other men fought not to laugh louder.

Hensley turned to them with a furious look, and the laughter stopped. He took a step closer to Cole and stared into his face. "I should shoot you right now."

"Then I'd miss the show of you using that tool of yours," Cole said with a grin. "This thing." He thrust his knee into Hensley's crotch. The red-head was lifted off the ground. The others were caught by surprise at their leader's collapse. Cole grabbed the closest one's wrist and twisted the arm backwards, forcing the gun free. A fist put the man to the mud.

The smack of cold steel on Cole's jaw was the last thing he felt.

Chapter Thirteen

Impending strangulation brought Cole out of his daze. Instinct made him struggle against the pain, tightening the strap looped around his neck. Every motion of his arms choked him. Reflex arched his back, letting him gasp air.

"Hey Carl, he come to," shouted a man from behind.

Blue sky was all he could see while bent backward on his knees. His right wrist, bound behind his left shoulder blade, tugged at the slackless strap, increasing the pressure on that side of his neck. He found the same result moving the other wrist. Coughing dug the wet rawhide deeper into the skin; suppressing the urge allowed the pooling saliva into his windpipe.

Gagging shortened the loop, tearing his eyes.

A head poked out of the blue sky. Hensley's grinning face emerged from the blur. "Hurt, don't it?"

Cole restrained any motion, though he had thoughts of personally showing the red-haired man how much agony it caused.

"Once saw a Mexican hog-tied like this by the Apache. Them fellows really know what hurts a man. Now, when Pete there finishes lacing the rest of it to your ankles, that rawhide will start drying, and it'll get littler. Then we'll see how long till your back gives out. If you fall over on your side, you probably break your neck right there. If you fall on your belly, well then, we'll see how long it takes before your legs get weak. When they do, then you just slowly hang yourself. The tale was that Mexican stayed like that for three days. The boys don't think you'll last that long," he said, ending with a wink. "But I'm betting on you."

"Carl," Cole gurgled through the saliva.

Hensley eagerly knelt to hear a plea for mercy.

Cole spit in his face.

Hensley wiped the spittle from his cheeks and drew his revolver. He stopped his thumb from pulling back the hammer. "No you don't." He shook his head. "It's not going to be that quick."

The stomping of hooves on the ground approached. Hensley moved out of sight.

Cole closed his eyes to concentrate. He

couldn't decipher what was said, but he recognized the voice. A moment later a horse snorting at his face forced his eyes open. Claire sat on the roan, her hands tied to the horn.

A sorrowful frown etched her face. She said, "I'm sorry. I'm so sorry." Her horse moved her out of view and Hoyt Larsen appeared.

"My, my. I guess you're not so tough after all. It is comforting to know my late partner's wife has such affection for you. It will make the job of her joining him that much easier."

Cole lurched up, but his bondage reminded him there was nothing he could do for her now. Larsen moved from Cole's view.

"You got the money yet?" he heard Carl ask.

"Not yet. There's still a matter Mrs. Rhodes and I have to see to in Platte Falls."

"Now you hold on. You said once you had the woman that we'd get our share of the money. It'll take you two days to get to town and back. How do I know you're even coming back?"

"Don't be stupid, Carl. I'll have your money when we return."

"Yeah, well, maybe we ought to go along, just to be sure."

"What about him?" There was a short pause.

"Hey, Pete, you ain't done yet?"

"This damn piece is cut too short," Pete complained. "It won't hold the knot."

"Well, hurry up. We're leaving to go to town."

A few seconds passed, then Cole heard horses galloping away. The sound soon faded.

Now Pete's frustrated pant was all he heard. "They're leaving you, Pete," Cole choked out. "You'll lose them if you don't go now."

"Shut up. Damn it, I'll make this work." Pete grabbed Cole's arms and the strap collared his neck backward.

When the tension stopped, Cole slid his bound arms up his spine to wheeze in air. He felt a knife blade nicking at his skin as Pete's hands entwined his with more leather. He was bent so far down, he smelled the man's breath. A bead of sweat dangled from Pete's nose. It reminded him of the fight with the grizzly; he was that near it.

When he pushed his arms further up his back, the taut strap slackened. Lunging against the restraint, he sank his teeth into Pete's nose. Loud screams broke the silence. Pulling to free himself, Pete frantically punched at Cole's head and chest, but the pressure remained constant. The teeth pierced flesh and Cole tasted blood. It gushed into both their faces.

Pete screamed louder, his hands scrambling to find the strap to stop the attack.

Cole's jaw locked and his arms tingled; the lack of oxygen was robbing his strength. If he failed, Pete would surely shoot him; this was his only chance. He heard the crack of bone splintering over the scream. His teeth sank deeper into the collapsing nose. Cole strained to relax his jaw, releasing Pete to roll on the ground. Out of the corner of his eye he saw the man covering his face in anguish. With Pete stunned, Cole had to act fast. Already he recognized hooves beating the ground.

He pushed up on his legs; they were still free, but a piece of leather had been tied to both ankles. He tried to get to his feet, but his legs were too weak from lack of circulation. He couldn't lift the weight, so he lay out straight. Pete wiped the blood from his face. The injured man rolled to the right, turning his back.

Cole threw his legs high, to cast the tethered straps over Pete's head and pull him onto his back. Pete went for his gun. Cole swung his legs, looping the leather around his captive's neck, as it was around his own, then pulled one leg against the other. Pete dropped the gun and grabbed at the suffocating cord.

Cole's leg strength returned with the blood flow. He spread his feet so hard the rawhide started cutting into the boot. Pete kicked, punched, and wiggled to get away. Loud choking gags signaled the fight was about to end. As the man fought, each attempt to gain freedom became weaker. Seconds later his limp arms fell to the dirt.

The pounding of hooves through the earth grew stronger. Cole strained against the strap at his throat, rose to his knees, and moved over Pete's body. With his back on the dead man's chest, his fingertips scrambled around, feeling for the knife. He touched hair, cloth, metal buttons, and leather, then recognized the texture of a carved bone handle. He squirmed to get a grip. The pain of steel slicing into his thumb told him he had found the knife.

"Hey, Pete, you all right?" Hensley called out.

Cole grabbed the side of the blade and rubbed the edge against his bound left wrist. He moved the edge back and forth like a saw, enduring the cramps that seized his fingers. The twinge of the point poking into his flesh forced him to cut at the strap faster, knowing in a moment he'd be free or dead.

His arm drooped, allowing him to pull against the slackening rawhide without choking. The binding snapped and he pulled his left arm free. The knot on his right wrist was still tight, but he had no time to loosen it. He unlooped the strap from around his neck, coughed out the smothering mucus, and took a reviving breath.

Gunshots jerked his head around. Carl Hensley stood next to a tree, aiming his .44 right at him. Dirt puffed up near Cole's head. He hurled the knife, but the blade found the tree. He jumped to his feet and began running, but fell back down, his feet still tied to Pete's neck. He got to his knees when he felt the sting of lead grazing his back, then he heard the blast of the shot. He crept, dragging the dead body as he went. If he stopped to free himself, he'd be just as dead. He crawled on hands and knees, listening for more shots, but none came. He quickly turned and heard Carl's angry grunts at having to reload, and another sound, the rush of rapids.

He followed the sound to a cliff. He dug his fingers in the ground for speed. He gripped the edge and pulled his head over to see the distant river flowing through a canyon.

"Shoot him," Carl shouted.

With a shove, Cole fell over the side, pulling the corpse with him. He waved his arms vainly to gain control of the fall.

Pete's body dropped straight down, twisting Cole around feetfirst. Air rushed into his face as the churning waves filled his view. He plunged into the water, its frigid grip instantly collapsing his chest.

He tried to get to the surface for air, but couldn't kick his tied legs. The weight of the sinking body pulled him farther down. Sunlight gave way to the dark depths. The pressure began crushing his temples. He stretched his arms overhead and repeatedly stroked the water past him. The undertow pushed against him. He moved his arms faster in the panic to breathe. With every motion, the water became brighter. He strained to raise his knees, lightening the weight on his legs for a second, rose up, stroked again, and popped his head above the surface.

He huffed in air quickly, as if it would be his last chance to breathe. The current drove him downriver. Waves lapped into his mouth. Drops splashed in the air as he heard faint gunshots over the surging rapids. He stopped treading to look up at the men shooting at him from the cliff. The weight pulled him under again, washing the view away.

He swam with only his arms again, maintaining a level just below the surface. Bullets darted through the water, leaving a stream of bubbles. He reached down to release the human anchor, but immediately sank. He moved to regain his position below the waves. The river's force jostled him from side to side. His ribs ached from exhaustion, seizing the strength from his arms. He had to get to the surface, even if it meant dodging more lead. He flapped up furiously once more, and his head poked above the water.

He inhaled again, and looked up, but the men were gone and only trees lined the cliffs above. The current had carried him around a bend in the canyon. He began to sink. Treading water, he swam for the rocky bank with only his arms, but the current propelled him farther down the river. The piercing pain in his side slowed his efforts. All he could do was keep treading to stay above the waves.

The canyon walls passed by faster and a deafening roar grew in the distance. It was a sound he knew. He vainly fought to get to the side. The current pushed him near a boulder firmly stuck in the riverbed. Navigating into its path, he crashed into the jagged rock and grasped the moss-covered edge. The weight under him began to pull him forward. He moved his feet in an attempt to untangle the cord from the body below him. After circling his legs, the weight at last eased away from his feet.

Water splashed over the rock, eroding his clawed grip. His fingers plowed through the slime and he was again in the relentless current. The force was at its peak, and his attempts to swim to safety were futile. He was going over.

White water lifted his body to the surface, where the river flowed over a cliff. The force threw him beyond the falls and the roar fell silent as he sailed down into the mist.

The jolt punched the breath from his lungs. He didn't have the energy to fight for life, but the churn brought him to the top. The wash floated him down the stream to calm shallows. The slap of the chilled ebb awakened him to survival.

He stood, stumbling from the persistent strap around his boots. Angrily, he unlaced the swelled knot and flung the rawhide into the water. His soaked clothes stuck to his skin as he trudged through the silt. Exhaustion dropped him to one knee.

Loud shouts from men filtered out of the forest. There wouldn't be any rest. They were coming after him.

Chapter Fourteen

Three men walked down the wooded hill in search of their quarry. They carefully stepped from tree to tree as they neared the riverbank.

"Hey, Tom. You see anything?"

"Shut up, Ben," Hensley ordered. "He could be anywhere around here."

"I think we're hunting a dead man, Carl. Ain't no way he could have come through them falls and lived." Ben's voice fell silent at the wave of Hensley's hand as he pointed toward the falls. All three of them crept closer to the water's edge. Hensley raised his Sharps in the direction he had pointed.

"I told you he couldn't have made it through them falls. You're shooting at a body."

"Shut up, would you? He may be playing possum. This will make sure of it if he is." Hensley aimed the rifle and fired.

"He didn't move, Carl," Ben said, throwing his shortened double-barreled shotgun on his shoulder. "I told you he was dead to start with."

Hensley turned his angered face at Ben.

"Hey, Carl," Tom said. "Does it look like he's got a black vest on?" All three moved closer to the water. "What was Pete wearing today?"

"A black vest," Hensley growled. Ben laughed. Hensley backhanded him to the ground so hard he knocked his own hat off. "That's Pete out there, and you're laughing." Hensley stuck the Sharps muzzle at Ben, who made no move to reach for the fallen shotgun.

"Quit it, Carl," Tom shouted. "It's Cole we're fighting."

Hensley pulled the rifle from its aim and handed it to Tom. He picked up his hat while still staring down at Ben. "We're going to get Pete out of the water. You stay here and look for that murdering son of a bitch." Hensley and Tom walked back toward where they all had come from. "You see anything, you start firing." Hensley brushed the thin red hair over his balding head and put on his hat as he and Tom passed through the trees.

Ben stood and brushed the dirt and leaves from his clothes. He picked up the shotgun and walked carelessly around the trees. The double-barrel dangled from his hand. "Son of a bitch.

The only one I seen just punched me in the mouth," he muttered.

The crack of a brittle limb brought the shotgun stock to his hip. He cocked both hammers while cautiously moving toward the hill. He moved from side to side, looking for the source of the noise. His hat's brim covered his face from view with every step. The crown of his Stetson showed the stains of dust and sweat.

Another crack brought Ben's eyes up to the tree branches. A water drop splashed his nose just before Cole's boot heel slammed into his face. One barrel fired. Both men hit the ground. Cole jumped to his feet, as did Ben, who retrieved the shotgun and swung it around.

Cole slapped the barrel up. It fired again. The blast sent sparks singing his hair. His ears rang. Leaves fell like snow. Ben kicked Cole to the dirt, then he reached in his pocket for more shells. Cole swung his leg at the man's ankle, tripping him. The shotgun fell free.

Ben pulled a switchblade from his boot and lunged. Cole caught the arm with his left hand as Ben fell on top of him. The blade neared Cole's face. The man's weight brought it even closer. The sharp point nicked his cheek.

Cole turned his face away from the knife, looping his right arm behind Ben's, bending it back like the lever of a fulcrum. Cole pulled the arm harder. Ben dropped the knife, crying, punching at Cole to release him. A loud pop sounded and the arm dangled loosely from Ben's elbow. He stopped punching.

Cole gripped the switchblade.

Ben's cries grew louder, ceasing when the switchblade sliced across his throat.

"We're coming, we're coming," shouted Hensley, running through the trees, revolver drawn. Hensley spotted the kneeling Cole and stopped to shoot.

Cole hurled the knife at Hensley's chest. It plunged into his thigh.

Hensley jerked with the pain and the pistol discharged into the air, flying from his grip. He dropped on his back, revealing Tom with the Sharps rifle, raising it to his shoulder to fire.

Cole dove to the dirt. The shot whizzed over his head, exploding bark off a tree.

Cole got to his knees and grabbed the double-barrel. He pawed through Ben's bloody shirt pocket for ammunition.

Panic filled Tom's face and he dropped the single-shot rifle, yanked the knife from Hensley's leg, and ran at Cole, yelling like a wild man. Cole pulled out the shells and cracked open the breech.

Leaves crackled under Tom's charge. Cole raised the shotgun to empty the barrels of the spent shells. Tom brought the knife over his head.

Cole sank the buckshot into place. With his thumb over the hammers, he cocked both of them by swinging the shotgun up, latching the breech.

Tom dove at him.

Cole pointed the scattergun at the man's face and pulled both triggers, falling back from the blast.

The forest turned orange, then gray.

Cole's right hand tingled. He tried to look at it, but his arm felt like it had been torn off. He rolled over to his stomach and glimpsed the bloody fingertips. He got to his knees and saw smoke wisping from the shotgun. He rubbed his aching arm and peered over his shoulder at the decapitated body. Blood, parts of bone, flesh, muscle, scalp, and an ear lay strewn over the ground. He climbed to his feet and through the ringing in his ears heard Carl Hensley's screaming voice.

"You murdering son of a bitch! I'm going to kill you!" Hensley held his bleeding thigh as he crawled on his side. He swatted the leaves, vainly looking for his pistol.

Cole staggered to him.

Hensley tried to move faster, but cringed with every motion of his leg. Cole bent over him and Hensley flinched. Cole lifted the revolver from behind the injured man.

"Looking for this?"

Hensley grimaced as Cole aimed the pistol at him.

"Where's Larsen? What did he do with the woman?"

Hensley gritted his teeth. "Go to hell."

Cole stomped on the bleeding thigh. Hensley screamed in agony. "I didn't hear you! I said where is he?"

Hensley pushed against Cole's boot. "My leg, my leg!"

Cole aimed at the other thigh and fired. Blood splattered from the hole. Hensley's misery took his breath. He coughed uncontrollably.

"You're going to die, Carl. Just a matter of how quick."

Hensley kept coughing until the ratchet of the hammer made him raise his hands for mercy. He wheezed in air. "Larsen took her to town. To get the money."

"Who went with him?"

Hensley's anguish wouldn't let him answer.

Cole pointed the gun at Hensley's stomach. "Takes a long time to die from a slug in the gut."

Hensley choked out his words. "No one—No, Ed is with him. Ed, that's all."

The screams brought to Cole's mind the pain that Hensley had caused him. He put all his weight on the helpless man's leg.

"Oh, sweet Jesus!"

Inured to the man's suffering, Cole aimed at Hensley's red hair. "Tell him I sent you." When the shot's echo faded, there was silence.

Claire squinted into the western sun, thinking of what she had to do next to stay alive. Once they arrived in town, her lie would quickly be exposed. Reasoning with Hoyt Larsen seemed out of the question. His face had a hard, unemotional expression. He hadn't uttered one word to her during the ride, and she chose not to speak for fear of sparking his wrath.

She couldn't help wondering how John, the man she had loved, could have turned into a man like Larsen in the single year they had been separated. Besides a home, she and John once shared thoughts and ideas, plans for their future. They had been intimate as husband and wife. There were times that she was the happiest woman in Baltimore as Mrs. John Rhodes. Her affection for those memories was shattered by the terror she now faced.

Riders came galloping out of the sun's glare. As soon as she could focus, she saw dark blue uniforms with gold trim. The men reined their horses to a trot and approached.

Ed threw his coat over her bound hands. What had become the familiar clicking of gunmetal drew her eyes to Larsen. The barrel of his pistol under his coat could only be seen by her.

"Any words you say will be your last, Claire," he whispered.

"Good afternoon," the officer greeted him. He tipped his hat to Claire. "Madam."

She nodded without smiling.

"I'm Major Miles Perry. My men and I are pursuing a traitor. A man named Clay Cole. Some people call him the Rainmaker."

Claire's eyes widened.

"He was last seen in the town of Platte Falls and was heading this way, reportedly with a woman," he said, eyeing Claire.

Ed looked at Larsen.

"Why, yes," Larsen said with a slight grin, then a scowl. "That must be the same man who killed my partner, John Rhodes, and assaulted Mrs. Rhodes."

Perry nearly shouted, "Do you know where this man is?"

"Yes. He brought Mrs. Rhodes, John's wife here, to us, threatening to kill her if we didn't pay him a ransom. John tried to save her and that man shot him, killed him. I was in great fear for her life and mine until my workers jumped him and were able to get her to safety." Larsen chuckled. "I told my boys they could have a little fun with him before they put him on the end of a rope."

"Frontier justice is not what the law calls for, Mr. . . . ?"

"Larsen. Hoyt Larsen. This is Ed Lawton. And frontier justice is all that people have out here, Major. There is no formal law in these mountains. A man has to protect what is his." He paused, looking at Claire. "And his loved ones. You have to make examples of those who take what isn't theirs."

Claire closed her eyes. When she opened them, she saw Perry staring at her.

"Pardon me for saying so, but you don't look well, Mrs. Rhodes. Are you injured?"

She shook her head. "No, Major Perry. It's been a trying day. I would like—"

"She'd just like to get her things in town and rest," Larsen interrupted. "I apologize, but I want to hurry and get her to a doctor. You can imagine my concern for her, after being with that outlaw."

Perry nodded. "Yes, I understand. Where can I find Cole?"

"I own a mine a few miles west of here. If you hurry, they may not have finished with him yet."

"Then we'll be on our way." Perry tipped his hat to Claire once more and motioned his men to ride.

"Major Perry," Claire called out. "I don't think the Rainmaker is the man you want." She saw Larsen's coat move slightly as the major stopped his mount.

"I beg to differ, Mrs. Rhodes. He is the man I'm looking for." Perry took one last glance at her, then at Larsen. "Good day to you," he said, and galloped off with his men.

Claire's heart sank once the soldiers were distant. "That was very foolish," Larsen said. She turned to him, and reeled from his backhand.

Chapter Fifteen

Cole climbed up a hill through the forest floor's mud. He realized that if Claire was still alive, it wouldn't be for long. The distance to Platte Falls was a hard ride in one day, and if he was to get there to save her, it would have to be done at night.

There were three hours of light left when he reached the mine encampment. It appeared deserted. He cautiously made his way to the shack. Kicking in the door, he found the room vacant. Then he saw John Rhodes on the floor. He knelt over the body. Cold blood surrounded a bullet hole in Rhodes's chest.

An open door led to a room with a bed and little else. He rummaged for anything he could find that would help him. All he found was a stack of papers with government writing, a table, chairs, a stove, a shelf with a can of beans, and a fine sculptured mahogany box.

Opening it, he found two cigars, some matches, and, under a false bottom, a key. The only door was the one he'd kicked in, and it had no lock. He ran outside, searching for what the key would open. He found nothing in the front or the back of the shack. The only other place was the mine itself.

He walked into the shaft. Within a few steps, the afternoon's light vanished, leaving him blind. Every step echoed down the cavern. He was wasting precious time and had to turn around. With his last step, he stumbled. A hollow sound boomed through the darkness. Crouching down, he felt a wooden crate. He slid his hands around the edge until he felt a cold metal loop. He had found what the key would open.

His fingernails scratched at the metal, finally sinking in the keyhole. Taking the key in his other hand, he squeezed it into the lock and turned. The shackle came loose. The wooden lid creaked as it opened. The shape of long, firm cylinders, fine coiled twine, and the smell of sulfur renewed his hope of getting Claire back.

Cole walked back to the light. Creeping out of the shaft mouth with five sticks in each hand and a fuse looped over his shoulder, he raced back into the shack and put two of the smokes and the matches in his shirt pocket. He ran outside and started the long walk back to town when he was stopped by a distant neigh. He tracked the echo up the rim of the gully where he had first sighted the mine. The cool air wrapped around him when he topped the hill. The open field revealed the long grass he'd seen before and nothing else.

He trudged through the wet ground, wondering where Claire would be by now. An hour or better had passed since Larsen took her. The look in that man's eye was one he'd seen before, a look of greed. If it was her money that Larsen was after, then chances were they wouldn't be camping for the night; not if it meant delaying his grip on fifty thousand dollars.

A grief-stricken face, the last sight he'd had of Claire, kept flashing in his mind. He stopped. He saw her last when he was tied up, and it was also the last time he had heard horses.

He turned back, running through the grass toward the forest. Darting through the trees, he slowed to listen for another landmark. A distant roar of water rang through the surrounding cliffs. He ran again, now faster. Clumps of mud flew from his boots, striking his cheeks and forehead. The fallen leaves crumbled as he thrashed through them. The river was near.

His heel slipped on a log. As it rolled, it threw him on his back, down a hill. He reached for the trunk of a spruce to stop his fall, but the bark tore the skin on his fingers. He clutched the remaining explosives; if they were lost, so would be his plan to save Claire. His momentum increased with the steepness of the incline. Turning on his side to slow himself only made him tumble shoulder over shoulder. Finally, level ground stopped his roll.

Every previous sore ached tenfold, but there were no broken bones. He cringed when he stood, secured the fuse back on his shoulder, regripped the sticks, then noticed a carved bone-handled knife stuck in a tree. A quick glance, and he spotted the rawhide strap on the ground. The familiar rush of rapids beckoned from over the nearby cliff.

He peered into the thick brush. There was no motion in the shaded darkness. He whistled and a whinny was the response. He ran toward the sound. A gray flash came through the maze of trees lining the bottom of the hill. As he went farther, white pigment beamed through the dimming light. Black spots became more visible with every stride he took. The stench of horse hair loomed; it was the sweetest smell in some time.

He rubbed the Appaloosa's rump as he approached and patted its neck. The delight of finding his ride was heightened by the sight of his black hat, covering his holstered Colt and cartridge-filled gunbelt looped around the horn. He reached up to untie the reins, but found them drooped to the dirt.

"I'll be damned," he said with a grin, patting

the animal once more, then he climbed into the saddle.

He rode along the base of the hill to where the slope was least steep. The rumbling of galloping horses made him rein in. He pulled back into the cover of the forest, out of sight of the approaching riders. He recognized their formation in an instant. As they passed through the grassy field, the leader's shoulder patches couldn't be recognized, but the man's trimmed black beard was unmistakable. It had been three years since Cole had seen that face, but the memory was clear. The clanking of steel and iron brought back that Montana morning. Now, not only did he have the army trailing him, but they were led by the one man who personally wanted to parade him in front of a firing squad.

As they headed for the mine, Cole looked back in the direction from which they had come and thought of the friend he had left behind. Once they were out of sight, he spurred the Appaloosa on.

The horses trampled through the tranquil pond. Drops splashed into Claire's face. She reminisced on the peace she had known there. It was in its gentle caress she had dreamed of her future with John while trying to put from her mind the forbidden fantasy of being in another man's arms. Although it was only yesterday, it seemed years had past.

The jolt of the roan stepping on firm ground

brought her back to the present. Larsen pointed toward something just ahead. Both men spurred their horses, and the roan sped up. After a short distance they abruptly stopped and looked at the ground. Claire's view was blocked by their backs. When they dismounted, she saw what concerned them, a hand protruding from the loose dug soil. Larsen brushed the dirt away, exposing the shirt cuff she'd seen before, that morning in the cabin, where Cole had fought and killed two men who'd threatened both of them. Larsen scooped out the dirt and uncovered the pale corpse. The blood-crusted scar in the neck, the stringy hair sprouting from the crushed skull.

"That's Bill, for sure," Larsen said, while looking at the other grave. "I'll bet Frank is in that one. Is this that old nigger's place?" Ed nodded. "While we're here, we might as well finish what we sent those two idiots to do."

Panic ran through her soul; she couldn't watch another man die because of her. Then she saw the dangling reins of the roan. She kicked its flanks and clutched the horn to hang on. She heard Larsen scream her name, but didn't turn to see him. Her concentration remained on the small cabin coming up over the horizon.

"Jenks, run, run! They're coming right behind me! Run!" The roan brought her around to the front of the cabin. There was no smoke from the chimney. The door stood wide open but no one came outside. The mud was chopped up from numerous tracks. *He may have already left*, she thought.

Larsen and Ed would soon catch her.

She called twice more, but when there was no response, she looked to the thick forest and kicked at the roan. The horse reared up. She fell back, but her hands remained bound to the horn, stretching her arms, pinching her skin. She looked at the blood on her wrist. A steel blade from behind slashed through the rope and an arm circling her waist ripped her off the saddle. As she tried to turn, a palm pressed over her mouth. She was dragged to the side of the cabin. Her captor fell against the wall, pulling her to the dirt. In her terror, she looked at the only object in view, the black fingers clutched under her nose.

"No peep from you and I'll let you go."

She nodded and the pressure ceased.

"Who is it you brung with you this time?"

She looked around to see Jenks's welted face. She began to ask what had happened to him, but the pounding earth cleared her mind of that worry.

"Hoyt Larsen."

"Larsen!"

"Yes. Him and one of his killers, and they'll kill us if we don't leave."

"Where's your man? Why's Larsen wanting you dead? Where Cole be?"

She closed her eyes a second, then looked

into his. "No time to explain. We must go. Now."

He tried to rise, but winced with the motion. "I used up all the use of this leg gettin' you. I won't be going far, not with this."

She peered down at the blood-soaked pant-leg.

"Run around back," said Jenks. "I'll get him here for a while."

"No. You must come with me."

He shook his head, then turned his view over her shoulder.

"Get away from him, Claire," Larsen ordered.

She saw him and Ed still mounted, aiming their pistols at Jenks.

"No, please no. This man has done nothing to you."

"The others didn't either. I want what he has—this land. Now move, woman."

She shielded Jenks with her body. "You'll have to shoot through me to hit him."

Both men laughed. Ed cocked his pistol.

"No," Larsen commanded. "We still need her to get to the money."

"Don't want to be dying with no white trash on top of me. Come get her hide off."

Larsen nodded to Ed, who dismounted.

Claire sank away from Jenks, confused by what he told them. She looked at him and he winked.

Ed walked over and grabbed Claire's arm.

She resisted.

He regripped the arm for a better hold.

Jenks wrapped his arm around her waist. Another yank lifted both of them. The old black man fell back, pulling Claire down, making Ed stumble forward. With the man hovering over him, Jenks shoved Claire away and thrust the knife's blade into Ed's chest.

"And take this with you."

Ed gripped Jenks's hand in reflex, but the blood pouring from his body buckled his knees. While his life dripped away, he stared at Jenks. "You black bast—" He collapsed on Jenks, who grinned widely.

Two blasts tore open Jenks's shirt, and blood trickled from the holes. Pain filled the old black man's face.

"No!" Claire screamed.

"God damn it!" yelled Larsen as he watched the riderless horses gallop away.

Claire crawled over to Jenks. Pushing Ed's body aside revealed the blood-stained blade in Jenks's hand. He nudged the knife at her hand.

"Take it. Wait for the time," he mumbled. "You'll know when you'll need it." He looked up at the heavens. "Maybe I'll see you up there." He winked once more, but didn't open the eyelid, then closed the other. A second later his body sagged, and his head swung lifeless to the side.

"No, God. Not this man," she whispered as she hugged the old black man.

"Let's go, Claire. I've gotten over the loss of Ed." Larsen's voice was filled with hate. "I didn't need him anyway." In a louder voice, he yelled, "We're losing the light, and we'll be slow enough riding double."

"Please. Just one more moment." With her back to Larsen, she kissed Jenks's cheek and discreetly took the knife from his hand, thumbed the blade closed, and slipped it under her hem into her shoe.

Chapter Sixteen

"There's a dead man inside but no one else, Major." Sergeant Lewis walked out of the shack, staring into the face of his mounted superior officer. "But someone was here not long ago. There are fresh tracks leading from the house and the mine."

"Find some lanterns and make a search down the shaft," Perry ordered.

Lewis saluted and went about his duty. The four subordinates found kerosene lamps and carefully made their way into the mouth.

Perry surveyed the camp. He was so close to his objective, but now he could feel the trail becoming cold. He dismounted and entered the shack. The dried mud foot tracks crumbled as he stepped into the doorway. He walked over and felt John Rhodes's cold cheek.

It seemed strange to him that Larsen wouldn't have at least covered the body. The scene looked as if it had been left in a hurry, perhaps when Larsen left to care for his partner's wife. What looked to be land claims were carelessly stacked on a table. A chair lay on its side in the corner. He looked at shelves on the wall and saw an empty cigar box. Odd that would be a thought in a man's mind when considering the safety of a woman.

Perry recalled the despair on Mrs. Rhodes's face. Why would a woman express concern for a man who'd killed her husband and threatened her own life? But, being a female, her actions couldn't be judged as logical.

He was leaving the shack when he noticed dark mud streaked on the floor. He removed his glove and wiped some on his fingers.

It was moist. The trail might not be as cold as he thought.

"Sergeant Lewis," he called as he charged out of the cabin. There was no reply. He went straight to his horse, mounted, and called again.

An echoed voice boomed from the cavern. A moment later, Lewis walked into the sunlight.

"Someone was here just before we arrived. I have a hunch it was Cole. I want to turn back at once and catch up to the Rhodes woman. Our answer will be with her. Where are the others?"

Lewis pointed down the shaft. "Back in there, sir. It's hard to find your way. It's as black as night. But we did find something."

Perry took more interest.

"There's a box of dynamite down there. It's been unlocked and there's some missing."

The major's eyes widened. "Call the men to mount! I'm going on ahead!"

The open grave made Cole slow his horse. The sleeved arm sticking out of the dirt was the same one he had planted there two days before, but the unbroken flesh told him the disturbance was not from hungry scavengers. Jenks wouldn't have dug up the dead. The sight of the boot-and hoofprints made him draw his Colt. He nudged the Appaloosa, following the tracks up toward the cabin.

The silence brought him out of the saddle. He crept to the corner of the shack. A few steps took him around to the front. The porch rocker seemed as lonesome as a hound waiting for its master to return.

He cocked the gun's hammer and knelt below the shattered window. He quickly rose to glance inside. Twinkling hearth embers reinforced his worst fear. He stepped past the open door. He turned his head from the lingering stench of spoiled stew. While holding his breath, he backed out of the vacant shack. He walked to the other end of the porch, wiping his tearing eyes, then stopped at the angled view of a man's boots lying on the ground near the side of the house.

He ducked back behind the front wall. The boots seemed polished; nothing Jenks would own. He edged around the corner to see first the boots, then pants, then a red-stained shirttail and sleeve. It couldn't be Jenks.

He stepped out, fanning the Colt at the first blurry object. He dropped the gun to his side when he saw the body of his old friend.

"Oh no. Damn! God damn!" He took two steps and fell to his knees next to Jenks's body, which lay against the wall. The bloody streams from the bullet holes and the absence of a pulse on the cool skin choked Cole's throat. The other man's wounded chest confirmed what had happened a short while ago.

"Well, old man, your luck finally run out," he whispered. "I'm sorry I'm the one that brought it on you." He paused. "I'm beholdin' to you for all that you done for me. I might've been dead a long time back if it hadn't been for you. I always thought that I'd beat you to the grave, and damn you, it was just like you to have gotten yourself shot just to show me wrong."

He sniffed, thinking about the other dead body. It proved he was on the right trail, and not having seen Claire's body along the trail meant she must still be alive. The sun below the treetops signaled lost time. Larsen would keep her breathing until they reached Platte Falls, but Cole would never make it there in time at night. He had to catch up to them before sunset. He had been too late to help this friend. If he didn't leave now, he'd mourn another. He squeezed Jenks's hand. "You rest now, Lucious. I'll be back to do you right. I promise."

He climbed onto the Appaloosa and headed toward Danger Ridge.

Claire rocked from side to side with every step of the horse. She attempted to steady herself with one leg wrapped around the horn while Larsen's arms secured her waist.

As they crested a hill, they could see two riders in the distance. "Oh, hell. What now?" Larsen cursed.

Claire recognized the flaming red shirt immediately. It was the old Mexican Ramiro Fuentes and his son Miguel. A third horse trailed behind, carrying what looked to be the figure of a man with a serape tied tightly over his head and shoulders.

"Remember what happened last time you talked to strangers, Claire," Larsen whispered as they neared the two travelers.

Fuentes tipped his hat as they approached. *"Buenas tardes, Señora."* His face was drawn and full of sorrow, and he looked back at the body. *"Este es mi hijo, Casimiro."*

"Oh no," she softly sighed.

"What? You know them? You understand what they're saying?" asked the surprised Larsen.

"Yes." It was then Claire realized the advantage she now held over him. "It would be rude for me not to answer him. They will sense something is wrong."

"Okay. But if I see anything I don't like, you'll be the first to know it." She felt the Derringer barrel pressed against her spine.

"You have my sincere sympathy, Señor Fuentes. How did this happen?"

The old man pointed far behind him. *"We traveled past the town of Platte Falls to the mountains north. It began to rain heavily. We had to camp in the trees because the river was impassable. The next morning, we saw my son's horse near the river's edge, just standing there. We knew Casimiro was in danger. We searched up and down the river the entire day. When the river lowered, that is when Miguel sighted the body of his brother. Casimiro had fallen from his horse and become trapped in the brush that was swept into the water."* Fuentes crossed himself. *"I am grateful for your assistance in finding my son, Señora."*

"What did he say?"

Claire thought a moment. "He said his son drowned in the river. It has become flooded from the storm and is now impassable."

"God damn. Did he find a place to get across?"

"Yes, but it took an entire day to get there."

"Where is it? How do we get there?"

"Señor Fuentes," she said, trying to act calm. *"Please don't be alarmed, or this man will become angry."* The young boy, Miguel, discreetly eyed

Larsen. *"If you wish to repay any gratitude to me, please, now point to the east and then find the American soldiers that are riding south of here to tell them I am in great danger. And please, hurry. I will owe you my life if you do so."*

The Mexican raised his hand to the east, then tipped his hat. *"We will do as you have asked."*

"Muchas gracias, Señor Fuentes," she said as the Mexicans rode off quickly.

"What did he say?" asked Larsen as he watched them ride away.

"He said there are shallows to the east where we can pass." She feared that the Mexican's haste would pique further interest from Larsen.

"Why did they leave so fast?"

She took a deep breath. "The man lost his son, Mr. Larsen," she sniped. "He wants to bring him home for burial. Even you should be able to understand that."

He turned his view to the east. "It'll take us into the night going that way." He brought his mouth close to her ear. "It might give us time to get to know each other better, Mrs. Rhodes. And you'll find out what I understand." He kicked the roan and headed east.

Cole followed the single horse tracks cut in the forest floor. The dimming light made them hard to see, but the direction toward Danger Ridge stayed true. Somehow he had to find a way to get there ahead of Larsen.

An opening in the trees gave him a chance to

move fast. He whipped the horse's flanks for speed. Once at full gallop, he saw two riders emerge from the distant trees ahead. He pulled his Colt; a habit when charged at by strangers. As they closed in, he raised the muzzle at the sky upon the sight of the red shirt one of them wore.

He reined in as they did. The old Mexican and his son rattled out their native tongue gibberish like the rapid fire of a Gatling gun. "Whoa," he shouted. "I don't know your lingo. Talk to me in American."

The old man turned to his son. *"Miguel, inglés."*

The boy hesitated, then spat out, "The—woman—is—trouble *grande*."

"You too, huh? Where is she?" The boy looked confused. Cole huffed in frustration. "Don—day?"

The boy pointed to where the two had come out of the trees, toward Danger Ridge. Cole stared at the distance. Their story had proved his hunch right; Larsen hadn't killed her yet. Both Mexicans started yakking their unknown words at him, but he paid no attention.

When he looked back at them, he noticed the corpse draped across the third horse. Cole motioned at the body. "Who is that?"

The boy's face became somber as he spoke. "Brother."

Cole peered at the ground a moment, then back at them. "Sorry to hear it." He holstered the Colt and offered his hand to the older man. "Thank—*gracias*."

The father shook his hand. He waved at the boy and nudged the Appaloosa to run. Following tracks would slow him. It was now a race to Danger Ridge.

He didn't turn when he heard the old Mexican's call. They were the only words he understood that old man say.

"Vaya con Dios."

Larsen slowed the roan. Its limping gait nearly threw Claire from the saddle; a fate she wouldn't have minded if it meant escape.

Larsen reined the horse to a stop. "Slide down."

She jumped to her feet and Larsen dismounted. He eyed her as he slipped the Derringer into his pocket. He hobbled around the roan and picked up a hind hoof.

Claire peered at the surrounding terrain cautiously, trying not to be noticed. It seemed only a few minutes had passed since she'd sent Señor Fuentes and his son after the soldiers. Her lie had given her time, but with the sun dipping down in the west, she would be alone with Larsen in the dark.

"What are you looking for?" Larsen asked with a grin.

His expression fueled her anger. She quivered as she answered, "Anyone that will help me."

He shook his head. "That would not be good. Not for you, anyway."

"And why is that?" He didn't answer. Her anger grew. "You murdered John. You're nothing but a cold-blooded killer. If it takes me the rest of my life, I will see you punished for his death."

Larsen looked up at her. "Don't forget. I was aiming at you, and I have a fresh load in both barrels." He continued cleaning the horse's shoe. "John's better off dead, anyway. From what he told me, something died in him the day he met you. Seems to me it was the part that made him a man."

She was enraged, but before she made her own curt response, her better sense squelched her tongue. He had already threatened to kill her. Instead, she slid one foot behind the other. "Oh, what else did my husband confide in you?"

"That he married you just to get back at your father, like he said. But when being married to you meant being under your daddy's thumb, he had to run."

"Is that when you stole his soul?"

Larsen chuckled while concentrating on scraping the stones free. "That was gone long before me. He had a mean streak in him that had been growing for some time. All I did was give him the way to put it to good use. Everything I did, he shared in. He had a taste for money as much as I did. He just stopped short at the things you have to do to get it out here."

Larsen went on with his story, but she

couldn't hear his words. She had taken flight through the brush. She pulled up her skirt to run free of the hem. Branches and leaves slapped her face. Larsen yelled angrily in the distance, and soon after she heard the clopping of hooves.

She ran as fast as she could. Each step sank deeper in the soft ground. She dashed into the thick bushes. Birds flew from the trees as she passed. Twigs and branches snapped behind her. When she glanced back to see if Larsen was close, her foot snagged on an exposed root. Her shoe slipped loose from the root as she tumbled down an embankment.

She rolled to the bottom of a leaf-covered gully. When she peeked up, the roan crashed through the thicket above her, pursuing a path away from where she lay. The canopy of branches hid the rider from view.

She kept still, afraid any motion would draw attention. She hushed her breath when the horse stopped. It stood firm. Its head lowered as it casually nibbled on the foliage.

She pushed herself to her feet, drew the knife from her shoe, and opened the blade. She stepped away through the gully.

The horse continued eating.

Her steps quickened. She glanced back but saw no movement from the roan. She looked straight ahead and headed back to where she had first started running, planning to double back to elude Larsen. She slowed down. Perhaps the soldiers would be near by now.

A limb hung low a few yards away. She could climb out of the gully and run to safety. She sprinted to it, grasped the bark, and pulled. One hand over the other, she climbed up the steep incline. She reached through the small sprouting branches. Suddenly, she felt a hand around her wrist.

A yank pulled her through the brush and she landed faceup on the rim of the embankment. A fist clutched her hair, stretching her head back. Larsen's evil scowl filled her sight. She jabbed the knife at his chest, but his hand stopped her arm with the point inches from its target. Larsen ripped the blade from her and threw it into the brush.

"Did you miss me?" He slapped her. "I missed you." He slapped her again.

Her stinging cheek filled her with rage. She spat in his face. He blinked it out of his eyes and pulled her hair back.

"Okay, missy," he growled. His fingers wrapped around her exposed throat and the pressure squeezed away her breath. "If that's the way you want it."

"You—won't—get—your—money," she gasped out. The pressure stopped, and slowly he released her throat.

"No more games. I was a fool to believe you were telling the truth about the river. Come on." He dragged her until she crawled and came to her feet. They slashed through the brush and he reclaimed the roan. "I'd better not have any trouble out of you," he warned, pulling the Derringer from his pocket. "Next time, the money won't save you."

About Robert

remained flat with _____. "I'd better not have any
complications." "If I go on telling the truth
_____ full pockets. "Next time, I'm doing it
your own way."

Chapter Seventeen

Cole slowed the Appaloosa to an amble. He scanned the ground, desperate to know of his success or failure. Dried hoofprints leading out of the pass provided his answer. He slowly rode on the narrow ledge and surveyed the rocky slope above him. There was no telling how many men were riding with Larsen, but however many, Cole had the one weapon that would even the odds. He dismounted and pulled out the five sticks of dynamite from his saddlebag.

He leaped from boulder to boulder up the steep ridge. The stench of rotting flesh stopped him. Looking down, he saw the scavenged skull of a man. A sweat-banded Stetson lay nearby. It served as a reminder of what happened to men who tried an ambush from these rocks. He continued up the slope. He peered down when he reached a point where the incline was too steep to climb. The Appaloosa appeared the size of a squirrel from this distance. He cut the fuse to splice in a second lead, then set it in three sticks and wedged them under a large boulder. He quickly stepped across the rocks until the fuse reached an end. There, he armed the remaining two sticks and wedged them as he had before. The trap was now set.

He strung the fuse down to the ledge and looped the excess over the saddlehorn. He didn't see any cover from which to shoot. With the explosive in the rocks, he would be left in the treeless open.

Claire's safety crossed his mind as well. If she had made it this far alive, he would have to be careful not to kill her himself.

While reloading the Winchester, a pattering of hooves brought his eyes to the distant forest. He couldn't make out who was riding the single horse toward him. He didn't have time to find cover. He steered the Appaloosa's bit at the bend around the opening and slapped its rump. The remaining fuse unreeled behind the fleeing animal. His panic had lost him his one advantage. It was too late to retrieve the horse. Cursing himself, he climbed up into the rocks.

It would have been foolish for Claire to try another escape. Larsen had a firm grasp of her waist as they rode. She peeked to find the Derringer at her back, and she felt his glance every time she moved her head. She had no confidence she could take the weapon from him. An attempt just might enrage an already unstable mind.

Distant peaks came into view between the trees. The sharp clack of hoof on stone broke the silence. The sparse brush remaining gave way to an open expanse. A rock-covered rim ascended into the sky with every jolting step of the mount. It was a sight she reluctantly recalled.

Larsen slowed the horse to a walk. As they entered the narrow ledge, she gazed at the towering pile of rock on one side, and the sloping wooded bluff down the other. The harrowing memory of the site overshadowed its beauty. She closed her eyes, trying to rid her mind of the fear.

The shout of a distant voice made Larsen rein to a halt.

"Somebody's up there," he said.

Claire opened her eyes. She grasped the horn tighter for balance against the horse's jittery moves. There was no movement in the rocks above, only a faint call.

"Let her go," echoed down.

Claire discreetly smiled. It quickly shrank upon the prod of the gun muzzle in her back.

"I don't believe it," Larsen muttered, then shouted, "Not a chance. She's worth a lot to me." He pulled harder at her waist, loosening her grasp on the horn.

"You can take the money. I just want the woman," came the reply.

"Maybe we can work a deal. Let me see you."

A moment passed. Claire squinted to spot a single dark figure rise from the white glare. Larsen reached into the saddlebag and drew out a spyglass. He yanked to expand the small telescope, but it wouldn't budge. Claire seized it from his fumbling hand, blew on the sections, and twisted it out to full length. She pointed it at the figure and her smile returned. There was Cole, a cigar clenched in his teeth. He took a match from his shirt pocket and with a strike of his thumbnail put flame to the cheroot.

Larsen jerked the glass from her eye and viewed the scene himself. A grimace creased his lips. "That son of a bitch is smoking my cigar."

"Let her go and I'll let you pass."

Larsen lowered the spyglass and looked at Claire. "And if I say no?"

"Then I'll bring down this ridge, and none of us will get what we want."

Larsen's arm tightened around her, and he spurred the horse. It bolted toward the far end of the ledge.

Claire was thrown back against his chest. She bounced in the saddle. Her hand slipped from the horn.

Larsen kept spurring to ride faster. The ledge became uneven, angling down toward the bluff.

Halfway through the pass, the increasing incline forced her further back. Larsen's grip eased to grab the slacking reins. Each stride jarred her more loose.

A shot rang out. Dust and pebbles flew in the air. The animal reared. Claire lost her balance and fell against Larsen, knocking both of them from the saddle. She crashed onto the stones, and rolled down the slope toward the bluff.

Cole's chest tightened when he saw Claire fall from the saddle. His shot might have gotten her killed. Jagged boulders blocked the line directly to her. He had to go down toward the opening where he had climbed up. He hurriedly jumped down on the rocks to the ledge, toward where Claire had fallen.

He heard a neigh, then the words, "Those Mexicans told me I'd find you here. Drop your weapon. You're under arrest."

He faced around to see Miles Perry on a horse, pointing a revolver at him and holding the Appaloosa's reins.

Cole tried to talk, but he was still biting on the cigar. He flicked it at Perry. "Let me go. There's a woman down there who needs help."

"That's not army business. I'm taking you back to Fort Lincoln for court-martial. I'll take you on top of this saddle or across it. Now drop the rifle."

Cole released the Winchester.

Perry waved his gun at him. "The side arm too."

"Miles, let me get to her. I'll come with you after that. She may still be alive."

"That doesn't matter to me," Perry said. "What about the three hundred men that lay buried at the Little Bighorn? The ones you killed? You weren't concerned for their lives."

"That wasn't my doing," Cole said as he approached the major.

"You warned the enemy of our advance. You got those troopers killed the same as if you had killed them all yourself. And I'm going to see you shot for it." Perry's grimace turned to a distraught frown. His eyes began to glisten.

Cole put his right hand over his gunbelt buckle and clasped it with his left. If he surrendered the Colt, then all hope of helping Claire would be lost.

"Miles," he said calmly. "It wasn't me that got them men killed. It was Custer that—"

"General Custer!"

"General Custer came up too quick. He would have had support in two days, but he couldn't wait. He had to have the glory all for himself. He wouldn't listen to what he was being told. He knew he was outnumbered and he still wouldn't listen. That's what wiped out them companies. I know, 'cause I was there."

"Exactly. That's why you're a traitor."

"I was trying to talk the Sioux and the Cheyenne into surrendering. I didn't know Custer was advancing."

"On whose authority?"

Cole hesitated. "The President of the United States."

The answer dropped Perry's jaw. "Liar! That weak drunkard wouldn't go against an army mission."

"It's true. It was supposed to be the army's mission to bring the Sioux back to the reservation without spilling blood. But your boy general wouldn't get elected herding them back behind a fence."

Perry's scowl returned. "Don't you talk about the general that—"

"Clay!" Claire's distant voice echoed.

Perry's eyes wandered to the cry. The revolver's aim drooped.

Cole released his right hand, drew the Colt, and fired from the holster top. The bullet struck Perry in the shoulder. He dropped his gun and fell off the saddle, crashing to the ground. Both horses scampered back to the opening.

Cole stood on the fallen revolver, hovering over the wounded major.

Perry held his bleeding shoulder, refusing to show the pain. The officer's curled lip seduced Cole into cocking the Colt.

The torment this man could bring could be squelched with a single shot. He sighted the barrel between Perry's disdaining eyes; better to be done with the deed quickly. A twitch would end it.

"Go on with it," Perry ordered defiantly.

Cole's gut told him to squeeze the trigger, but his head seized his finger. He had killed many men before, but he wasn't a murderer. He pulled the trigger, his thumb on the hammer, easing it against the chamber. "Someone's going to send you to hell, Miles," he said, holstering the Colt. "But it won't be me.

Visions of Claire on the bluff came to his mind. He picked up the service revolver and flung it away. Turning to locate the Appaloosa, he spotted soldiers riding at full gallop toward him.

A sizzling sound brought his eyes back to Perry, and he saw the major holding the cigar, sparks engulfing the fuse up into the rocks.

He ran to his horse. A whistle kept the Appaloosa from running. A blast rang out, dust popped in the air. He grabbed the reins, stepped in the stirrup, and swung up into the saddle. He spurred the horse toward the ledge.

Perry laughed while running at Cole. "I have you, you bastard," he screamed, grabbing at Cole's leg.

Cole booted him to the ground and headed into the smoky haze. He kicked the horse's flanks and lashed the reins against the rump. The animal's huffing breath and beating stride pounded into his ears. He saw the smoke drift from the rocks above. "Come on," he grunted.

He pumped the handful of mane for more speed.

Perry's voice cried, "No!"

Cole glanced back to see the soldiers following him on the ledge.

The ground shook.

The Appaloosa stumbled, but kept running. Rocks flew up from the top of the ridge as if shot from a cannon. Dust-bellowed lines emerged from the explosion. Boulders rolled down the slope.

Horses whinnied.

He peered back to see the soldiers desperately trying to turn around on the narrow ledge. The sound of men screaming shrieked over the rumbling. Stones pelted the ground like hail. One struck Cole's shoulder, jarring him around in the saddle. He glimpsed boulders pummeling the mounted soldiers off the ledge. The screams stopped.

The ground shook once more. The Appaloosa fell. Cole jumped from the saddle, rolling down the sloped bluff. He snagged a spruce to stop his fall. The landslide was heading for him. He jumped to grab a limb and pulled his belly over it. Rolling boulders slammed into the trunk. He looped his arms to hold on. The aching creak of wood slowly splitting filled his ears.

The spruce listed. The trunk cracked.

He closed his eyes as the tree fell. His breath left his body with the landing. He gasped to regain it. Dust filled his lungs. He coughed it out and tried to get up, but his leg shot with pain from the motion. He squinted through the lingering haze at the splintered wood lanced through the side of his right thigh.

Pebbles trickled between the rocks. The rumbling had stopped. He leaned against the fallen trunk. His throat stung from the dust he inhaled. The joints in his fingers would bend only halfway. His shoulder throbbed, and a knifing twinge ran down his side. He spat the dirt from his lips and through the ringing in his ears he heard a voice.

"Clay."

She was still alive. He twisted around, but couldn't see her through the trees. He pushed against the trunk to stand, but the agony from his wound stopped him. He took a breath, then another to fill his chest. He gripped the wood and extracted it from his leg. Blood ran to the ground. The sting slackened once the stick was pulled free. He looked at the jagged red point and threw it over the rocks. He tucked his left leg under his backside and stood.

Another call echoed.

He stepped out over the rubble toward it.

Claire clawed the dirt, steadying herself on the bluff's edge. She couldn't peek at the canyon's depth behind her.

Cole called her name. She saw him coming. The thought gave her the courage to stand. His face glimmered in the twilight as he walked through the trees.

A shot rang out. She saw Larsen standing on a boulder, pointing his Derringer at Cole as he neared.

Cole returned fire, but the bullet ricocheted off the rock.

Larsen looked at her and jumped down. She froze. He hobbled at her as Cole came out of the trees and fired again.

The shot missed.

Larsen's arm wrapped around her throat and he put the muzzle at her temple.

Cole aimed at his head, then pointed the Colt away.

"Drop your gun. Drop your gun or I'll kill her, I swear."

She quivered, trying to balance herself in Larsen's weighted grasp.

Cole held the Colt.

"Do it!"

The Colt drooped slowly to his side, then to the ground.

"No, Clay. He'll kill us both," she said through shortened breath.

Cole nodded. "I know."

Larsen cackled. "I guess you two did became more than friends on the way here."

The pressure at her temple stopped. Larsen's arm stretched out and pointed the pistol at Cole, whose face appeared to be resolved to take the bullet.

Her heart pounded, pressing her chest to the brooch pinned inside her blouse.

Larsen pulled back the hammer.

She reached inside her blouse and gripped the ornament as a knife. "No!" she yelled. Thrusting her arm down, she jabbed the pin into Larsen's leg.

His arm slipped from her throat and clutched her stabbing hand. The Derringer fired as he fell backward.

She was twisted around by Larsen's collapse, his grasp firm on her wrist.

He grabbed her hand and pulled the brooch free. His boots slipped on loose stones, sending him down the side, one hand gripping the rocky edge of the cliff and the other latched onto her arm.

His bulging eyes stared at her. A strained wail boomed from his open mouth. He flexed his arms to climb. He propped his elbow against the edge and reached for her. "Help me. Oh dear God, help me."

She was pulled closer to the edge. Her eyes filled with the sight of the vast chasm.

His nails scraped the rocks, but he lost his grip. Only her arm kept him from falling.

"Help me. Please!"

Tears streamed down her cheeks. She screamed while she was being dragged further over the edge.

Larsen's grasp slid from her wrist to her brooch-bulged hand.

A green-sleeved arm grabbed her forearm. "Let it go!" shouted Cole.

Claire released the conscious desire to keep the brooch. Her hand relaxed, the ornament fell free.

Larsen's grip slipped from her hand. "No!" he screamed. His face disappeared over the edge. His cries grew faint, then ceased.

Cole still held her arm as she looked up. He gently lifted her to her feet.

She wrapped her arms around him and sobbed in his shirt. As she gulped in breath, she heard his low voice.

"He won't hurt now."

Chapter Eighteen

The engine's black smoke drifted into the sky, shrouding the station from sunlight. Claire walked out on the platform toward the train. A porter carted a large trunk and placed it in front of her. She forced a smile to thank him and paid him a gratuity as he left.

She glanced at her reflection in the train car window. The scarlet dress was the darkest one she had brought, but the white lace lapels and the matching hat didn't fit the image of a recent widow.

She touched the last reminder of her marriage to John Rhodes and took a deep breath to hold the tears from marring her face. She wasn't going to allow that painful memory to destroy her regained pride. She had fulfilled her duties as a wife, and had proved that by coming west to join the man she'd vowed to honor; something that most women she knew would never have attempted. Now that part of her life was over. She removed the gold band from her left hand to place it now on her right ring finger. After a moment's thought, she tossed it on the tracks.

The hollow sound of footsteps on the wooden boards turned her attention back to the station. A smile creased her face when she saw Clay Cole standing in front of her, holding her blue taffeta dress.

"I don't promise much, but I keep those that I make." He held out the dress and she took it into her arms.

She fondly looked at it, then at him. "I didn't know if I would ever see you again."

"There was another promise I had to keep. I needed the two days to see that a friend got buried decent. Christian like."

There was a silence as she thought of the other man who had risked his life for her. "I liked him very much, and I will miss him. He was a kind old gentleman, even if he didn't like showing it."

"I think he took a shine to you too."

She gently wiped the tear from the corner of her eye, then looked at the dress again. She knelt to open the trunk. "It's time to return everything to its place." Propping the lid up, she folded the dress and placed it inside, next to the banded gold certificate notes stacked on the bottom. "Myself included."

He waved his finger at the money. "You be careful not to show that. Still a lot of people would like to have use of it."

"For all the misery it has given me, I would just as soon give it away." She looked up at him. "It could be yours if you wanted what went along with it."

He shook his head. "That much money would cause me the same type of trouble it did you. Anyway, you earned the right to keep that money. Can't think of many men that would have put up with, or could have done what you did. You're a brave woman, Claire."

She closed the trunk lid and latched it shut. Rising, she gazed into his blue eyes. The scar above his eyebrow had healed, blending into his sun-reddened face. "I suppose you'll go collect your money in Nobility now."

He nodded. "Got to try. But I was supposed to have been there to wire yesterday. Don't know if he'll send the money or Pinkertons."

"You could have been there yesterday." Her statement had the tone of inquiry.

He pushed his hat up, revealing the smile that she had always enjoyed. "Then I couldn't have brung you the dress, or said good-bye."

She thought of a question, but hesitated to ask.

"The train leaves in five minutes, folks," the

conductor interrupted as he walked by, checking his pocket watch.

Claire peered at the ground, drawing the courage to say what she felt. "You could collect your money in person." She raised her gaze to him.

"What, me in a big Eastern city?"

She nodded, careful not to appear over-anxious with the suggestion. "I'm sure my father would want to meet the man he sent to protect his daughter."

He stared off at the clouds, then shook his head. "It wouldn't mix. Besides, that would put me closer to the people in Washington I'd just as soon not run across."

She nodded; on one more point she found herself in agreement with him, and she still hated it.

Lieutenant Andrew Moore led the six troopers under his command to the Platte Falls Palace. Ordering the men to dismount, he reined his horse to the post. He removed his gloves and brushed the dust from the three-day ride off his uniform, while peering at the small town he had left in the middle of a rainy night because of the obsession of a superior officer.

"Corporal Turner," Moore called out.

A young enlisted man came to his side and addressed Moore with the proper salute. "See the men get six days rations for the ride to Fort Lincoln. The troop will leave in one hour." The young soldier's face looked confused at the order. "Any questions, Corporal?"

"Begging the Lieutenant's pardon, sir. But Major Perry's party . . . well, sir, should we leave without them, sir?"

"Are you making decisions for the troop now, Corporal?"

"No sir," Turner answered, loudly and respectfully. He turned about-face and took a step back to the other soldiers.

"Wait." Moore's command halted the corporal. He took no comfort in belittling men, as did Perry. "We were to meet Major Parker four days ago and we failed. We haven't seen Major Perry in three days, and I cannot expose these men and myself to the risk of court-martial if we don't report back to Fort Lincoln as soon as possible. Major Perry took it upon himself to pursue this man called the Rainmaker. I regret having to leave without him and the others, but we must obey our orders." He turned to look at the attentive corporal. "Any further questions?"

"No sir."

"Then carry out my orders." The corporal saluted and called to the other men. Moore stood alone in the street, pondering what he had just said. He sensed there would be silent discontent among the men for leaving without their true commanding officer, but he was steadfast in the decision. He had a career to think about.

He slapped his gloves on his thigh and began to turn around when something caught his eye.

He stared at a saddled Appaloosa reined near the train station. He couldn't place why he should take notice of the horse, but there was something in the back of his mind that told him not to ignore this seemingly trivial discovery.

"Corporal Turner," he called, while maintaining sight of the animal. Turner returned to his side. "What is there about a gray Palouse that reminds me of this town?"

The young soldier thought for a moment, then snapped his fingers. "That old drunk, the night we rode in, he said something about a gray Palouse and the . . ." His speech slowed. ". . . the Rain-ma-ker." They both looked down the street at the horse.

Moore took a deep breath. He had already expressed his views on this matter, but the remedy to this debacle could be within his grasp. It was worth a chance. After all, what would his career record read like with the capture of a traitor the army wanted so badly? "Assemble the men. We'll have a look."

"All aboard," the conductor shouted.

Claire nodded at the announcement. "Time to go."

"Damn, I almost forgot," said Cole as he pulled a small canvas sack from his shirt pocket. "I—uh, I'd feel pretty sorry if you had to leave this behind."

She smiled as she took the sack, but before she opened it she heard the huffing roar of the engine. She scanned for a porter. "I must still have my trunk loaded in the baggage car."

Cole sheepishly grinned and knelt backward to the huge trunk, grabbed the thick leather handle, and lifted it on his back.

"With what you got in here, you're better off having it in sight."

A porter came out of the car and stopped, awestruck at the scene of this one man carrying the load up the iron steps.

Dropping it with a thud, Cole stared at the small man, whose mouth was agape. "See this gets to the lady's seat."

The porter quickly nodded. Cole stepped back down. It took him a moment before he spoke to her. "Well now, you take care of yourself."

"Me? It is I who should be saying that to you. You will be in my thoughts and my prayers. Do be careful on your trip."

"It'll be nice knowing that you'll remember me."

She smiled. "Clay Cole, I can't imagine forgetting you. Not as long as I live." The train's whistle screamed the final warning of departure. She climbed onto the second step of the iron landing and turned to him. His blue eyes beamed from the shade of his hat straight into hers. She offered her hand. He didn't take it. "Well, this is good-bye. Thank you for my life. And thank you for being my friend."

He leaned toward her, gliding his hands along the sides of her bust to find the seams of her sturdy corset. She didn't resist the advance. He gently pulled her closer, guiding her lips to his. His kiss was warm and more than friendly as she fell into his firm embrace. Her arms slid over his broad shoulders and around his neck. Her heart pounded and her knees slightly buckled. A jolt separated them, their lips the last to part. The train moved forward.

She looked upon him for the last time. He stood motionless at the end of the platform. His face was hidden by the brim of his hat, as when she had first seen him, only now she knew the man beneath the shadow.

Steam flying by clouded her view. When it dissolved, she felt the speed of the train increase as it left the station. Her journey home had begun.

She watched his figure shrink in the distance while she reflected on her experience in the West. It had proven to be the barbaric world her father and others had said it would be. She had discovered that life in this wild land was one continuous act of survival. She herself had escaped death many times while at the mercy of men she didn't know. She'd been witness to the death of many, one of whom she had once loved.

She realized that she herself was a survivor, and that she could fall in love with a man she hadn't planned on. A man Westerners called the Rainmaker, and she knew as Clay Cole.

The jostling of the train awoke her from her

daydream. She noticed she still held the canvas sack. Untying the strings, she spread the opening and pulled out her gold-mounted ruby brooch.

She looked up in hopes of seeing him once more. The engine bellowed steam again. When it cleared, he was gone.

WILL HENRY

WHO RIDES WITH WYATT

"Some of the best writing the American West can claim!"
—*Brian Garfield, Bestselling Author of Death Wish*

They call Tombstone the Sodom in the Sagebrush. It is a town of smoking guns and raw guts, stage stick-ups and cattle runoffs, blazing shotguns and men bleeding in the streets. Then Wyatt Earp comes to town and pins on a badge. Before he leaves Tombstone, the lean, tall man with ice-blue eyes, a thick mustache and a long-barreled Colt becomes a legend, the greatest gunfighter of all time.

BY THE FIVE-TIME WINNER OF THE GOLDEN SPUR AWARD

___4292-4 $3.99 US/$4.99 CAN

Dorchester Publishing Co., Inc.
P.O. Box 6640
Wayne, PA 19087-8640

Please add $1.75 for shipping and handling for the first book and $.50 for each book thereafter. NY, NYC, and PA residents, please add appropriate sales tax. No cash, stamps, or C.O.D.s. All orders shipped within 6 weeks via postal service book rate. Canadian orders require $2.00 extra postage and must be paid in U.S. dollars through a U.S. banking facility.

Name_____
Address_____
City_____State_____Zip_____
I have enclosed $_____ in payment for the checked book(s).
Payment <u>must</u> accompany all orders. ☐ Please send a free catalog.

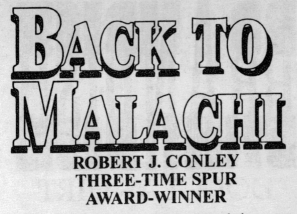

BACK TO MALACHI

ROBERT J. CONLEY
THREE-TIME SPUR
AWARD-WINNER

Charlie Black is a young half-breed caught between two worlds. He is drawn to the promise of the white man's wealth, but torn by his proud heritage as a Cherokee. Charlie's pretty young fiancée yearns for the respectability of a Christian marriage and baptized children. But Charlie can't forsake his two childhood friends, Mose and Henry Pathkiller, who live in the hills with an old full-blooded Indian named Malachi. When Mose runs afoul of the law, Charlie has to choose between the ways of his fiancée and those of his friends and forefathers. He has to choose between surrender and bloodshed.

__4277-0 $3.99 US/$4.99 CAN

Dorchester Publishing Co., Inc.
P.O. Box 6640
Wayne, PA 19087-8640

Please add $1.75 for shipping and handling for the first book and $.50 for each book thereafter. NY, NYC, and PA residents, please add appropriate sales tax. No cash, stamps, or C.O.D.s. All orders shipped within 6 weeks via postal service book rate. Canadian orders require $2.00 extra postage and must be paid in U.S. dollars through a U.S. banking facility.

Name_____
Address_____
City_____State_____Zip_____
I have enclosed $_____ in payment for the checked book(s).
Payment <u>must</u> accompany all orders. ☐ Please send a free catalog.

BRANDISH

DOUGLAS HIRT

FIRST TIME IN PAPERBACK!

Captain Ethan Brandish has finally given up his command of Fort Lowell, deep in Apache territory. But the vicious Apache leader, Yellow Shirt, has another fate in store for him. He and a group of renegade warriors attack a stage station and ride off just before Brandish arrives. But the Apaches are still out there—watching and waiting—and Brandish must risk his own life to save the few wounded survivors.

___4323-8 $4.50 US/$5.50 CAN

Dorchester Publishing Co., Inc.
P.O. Box 6640
Wayne, PA 19087-8640

Please add $1.75 for shipping and handling for the first book and $.50 for each book thereafter. NY, NYC, and PA residents, please add appropriate sales tax. No cash, stamps, or C.O.D.s. All orders shipped within 6 weeks via postal service book rate. Canadian orders require $2.00 extra postage and must be paid in U.S. dollars through a U.S. banking facility.

Name_____
Address_____
City_____State_____Zip_____
I have enclosed $_____ in payment for the checked book(s).
Payment <u>must</u> accompany all orders. ☐ Please send a free catalog.

DON'T MISS OTHER CLASSIC *LEISURE* WESTERNS!

McKendree by Douglas Hirt. The West had been good to Josh McKendree. He had built a new life for himself with a loving wife and a fine young son—but halfbreed trapper Jacques Ribalt took it all away from him when he slaughtered McKendree's family over a simple land dispute. Now, McKendree has only one thing left—a need to make Ribalt pay for what he did. And the West is just a place where his family's killer is hiding. And McKendree will see justice done...or die trying.

_4184-7 $3.99 US/$4.99 CAN

Mattie by Judy Alter. Young Mattie, poor and illegitimate, is introduced to an entirely new world when she is hired to care for the daughter of an influential doctor. By sheer grit and determination, she eventually becomes a doctor herself and sets up her practice amid the soddies and farmhouses of the Nebraska she knows and loves. During the years of her practice, Mattie's life is filled with battles won and lost, challenges met and opportunities passed.

_4156-1 $3.99 US/$4.99 CAN

Dorchester Publishing Co., Inc.
P.O. Box 6640
Wayne, PA 19087-8640

Please add $1.75 for shipping and handling for the first book and $.50 for each book thereafter. NY, NYC, and PA residents, please add appropriate sales tax. No cash, stamps, or C.O.D.s. All orders shipped within 6 weeks via postal service book rate. Canadian orders require $2.00 extra postage and must be paid in U.S. dollars through a U.S. banking facility.

Name_____
Address_____
City_____State_____Zip_____
I have enclosed $_____ in payment for the checked book(s).
Payment <u>must</u> accompany all orders. ☐ Please send a free catalog.

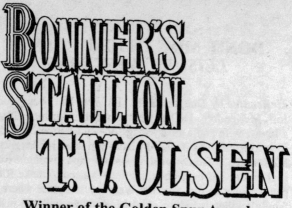

BONNER'S STALLION
T. V. OLSEN

Winner of the Golden Spur Award

Bonner's life is the kind that makes a man hard, makes him love the high country, and makes him fear nothing but being limited by another man's fenceposts. Suddenly it looks as if his life is going to get even harder. He has already lost his woman. Now he is about to lose his son and his mountain ranch to a rich and powerful enemy—a man who hates to see any living thing breathing free. That is when El Diablo Rojo, the feared and hated rogue stallion, comes back into Bonner's life. He and Bonner have one thing in common...they are survivors.

___4276-2 $4.50 US/$5.50 CAN

Dorchester Publishing Co., Inc.
P.O. Box 6640
Wayne, PA 19087-8640

Please add $1.75 for shipping and handling for the first book and $.50 for each book thereafter. NY, NYC, and PA residents, please add appropriate sales tax. No cash, stamps, or C.O.D.s. All orders shipped within 6 weeks via postal service book rate. Canadian orders require $2.00 extra postage and must be paid in U.S. dollars through a U.S. banking facility.

Name_____
Address_____
City_____ State_____ Zip_____
I have enclosed $_____ in payment for the checked book(s).
Payment <u>must</u> accompany all orders. ☐ Please send a free catalog.

SPUR AWARD-WINNING AUTHOR

GORDON D. SHIRREFFS

Southwest Drifter. Wes Yardigan's luck is beginning to run dry. It kept him alive all the years he's drifted the territory, a stubborn saddle tramp chasing the wind. Now he wants to settle down, and has even managed to scratch up a stake—just in time for the Indians to sweep down out of the hills and leave him with nothing but his own thick skin. One more day in this blistering country and he won't even have that. But Yardigan's luck hasn't quite run out. Two men ride in with a curious proposition—a deal that will give him a chance to stake himself again. And after he agrees, he realizes he should have taken his chances in the desert.

_4207-X $3.99 US/$4.99 CAN

Dorchester Publishing Co., Inc.
P.O. Box 6640
Wayne, PA 19087-8640

Please add $1.75 for shipping and handling for the first book and $.50 for each book thereafter. NY, NYC, and PA residents, please add appropriate sales tax. No cash, stamps, or C.O.D.s. All orders shipped within 6 weeks via postal service book rate. Canadian orders require $2.00 extra postage and must be paid in U.S. dollars through a U.S. banking facility.

Name_____
Address_____
City_____State_____Zip_____
I have enclosed $_____ in payment for the checked book(s).
Payment <u>must</u> accompany all orders. ❏ Please send a free catalog.

THE WORLD'S MOST CELEBRATED WESTERN WRITER!

MAX BRAND

Donnegan. He comes from out of the sunset—a stranger with a sizzling six-gun. Legend says that he is Donnegan. And every boomtown rat knows he has a bullet ready for any fool who crosses him. But even though the Old West has fools enough to keep Donnegan's pistols blazing, the sure shot has his sights set on a certain sidewinder, and blasting the deadly gunman to hell will be the sweetest revenge any hombre ever tasted.

_4086-7 $4.50 US/$5.50 CAN

The White Wolf. Tucker Crosden breeds his dogs to be champions. Yet even by the frontiersman's brutal standards, the bull terrier called White Wolf is special. And Crosden has great plans for the dog until it gives in to the blood-hungry laws of nature. But he never reckons that his prize animal will run at the head of a wolf pack, or that a trick of fate will throw them together in a desperate battle to the death.

_3870-6 $4.50 US/$5.50 CAN

Dorchester Publishing Co., Inc.
P.O. Box 6640
Wayne, PA 19087-8640

Please add $1.75 for shipping and handling for the first book and $.50 for each book thereafter. NY, NYC, and PA residents, please add appropriate sales tax. No cash, stamps, or C.O.D.s. All orders shipped within 6 weeks via postal service book rate. Canadian orders require $2.00 extra postage and must be paid in U.S. dollars through a U.S. banking facility.

Name_____
Address_____
City_____ State _____ Zip_____
I have enclosed $_____ in payment for the checked book(s).
Payment <u>must</u> accompany all orders. ☐ Please send a free catalog.

GORDON D. SHIRREFFS

Recipient of the Owen Wister Lifetime Contribution Award

Now He is Legend. Ross Starkey is a loner, a drifter, a fighter who lives by his guns and rides wherever the money is—to range wars in the north, to revolutions south of the border, to any renegade who has the right price. Now Starkey wants out, and there is just one thing that stands in his way—a man they call the Tascosa Kid. Ross' only friend, his partner, and now his bitter enemy, the Tascosa Kid will keep Ross from hanging up his guns...even if it means killing him.
_4124-3   **$3.99 US/$4.99 CAN**

Bugles On the Prairie. In lawless towns from Santa Fe to Calaveras County, Ross Fletcher will need every ounce of courage and cunning he possesses to avenge the death of his brother, stop a deadly ambush, and rescue a beautiful woman held captive under the searing Arizona sun.
And in the same action-packed volume....
Rio Bravo. Somewhere beyond the Rio Bravo, two women are held hostage in the wilderness by an Apache chief who plans his master stroke against the white eyes. And when Lieutenant Niles Ord, U.S. Calvary, throws his frontier troop onto the bloody scales of battle, will he tip the balance toward victory—or go down fighting?
_4078-6**(Two complete Westerns in one volume!)**$4.99 US/$5.99 CAN

Dorchester Publishing Co., Inc.
P.O. Box 6640
Wayne, PA 19087-8640

Please add $1.75 for shipping and handling for the first book and $.50 for each book thereafter. NY, NYC, and PA residents, please add appropriate sales tax. No cash, stamps, or C.O.D.s. All orders shipped within 6 weeks via postal service book rate. Canadian orders require $2.00 extra postage and must be paid in U.S. dollars through a U.S. banking facility.

Name_____

Address_____

City_____State_____Zip_____

I have enclosed $_____ in payment for the checked book(s).

Payment <u>must</u> accompany all orders. ☐ Please send a free catalog.

PB
W
12-98

ATTENTION WESTERN CUSTOMERS!

SPECIAL TOLL-FREE NUMBER
1-800-481-9191

Call Monday through Friday
10 a.m. to 9 p.m.
Eastern Time
*Get a free catalogue,
join the Western Book Club,
and order books using your
Visa, MasterCard,
or Discover*®

Leisure
Books

GO ONLINE WITH US AT DORCHESTERPUB.COM

D